NANCY'S NEXT HOT TOPIC?

As Nancy stood in the middle of the dwindling party, deciding what to do next, she felt a hand on her shoulder. When she turned she found Jake standing there in a sport coat, pressed denim shirt, and jeans.

"All dressed up and no place to go, huh?" Nancy said, eyeing his sport coat. It was the first time she'd seen him in anything but a wrinkled shirt. He'd even polished his boots. Nancy thought he looked pretty sexy.

"Well, *you* look beautiful," he said, beaming. "It seems a shame to waste that outfit, since this party's turned out to be a bust. And, as you can see, I went to *great* lengths to make myself presentable."

"Are you *suggesting* something?" Nancy laughed.

"Only if you're going to say yes," Jake replied. "After all this effort, I don't think I could take a rejection."

NANCY DREW ON CAMPUS™

Available from ARCHWAY Paperbacks

Nancy Drew
on campus™ #5

Secret Rules

Carolyn Keene

AN ARCHWAY PAPERBACK
Published by POCKET BOOKS
New York London Toronto Sydney Tokyo Singapore

This book is a work of fiction. Names, characters, places and inci-
dents are products of the author's imagination or are used ficti-
tiously. Any resemblance to actual events or locales or persons,
living or dead, is entirely coincidental.

AN ARCHWAY PAPERBACK *Original*

An Archway Paperback published by
POCKET BOOKS, a division of Simon & Schuster Inc.
1230 Avenue of the Americas, New York, NY 10020

Copyright © 1996 by Simon & Schuster Inc.
Produced by Mega-Books, Inc.

ISBN: 0-671-52746-0

First Archway Paperback printing January 1996

10 9 8 7 6 5 4 3 2 1

NANCY DREW, AN ARCHWAY PAPERBACK and colophon
are registered trademarks of Simon & Schuster Inc.

NANCY DREW ON CAMPUS is a trademark of
Simon & Schuster Inc.

Cover photos by Pat Hill Studio

Printed in the U.S.A.

IL 8+

CHAPTER 1

W hat happened to you guys?" Nancy Drew asked as she watched Bess Marvin and Eileen O'Connor stumble into the Thayer Hall cafeteria. Drenched and mud stained, the two girls slogged over to the table where Nancy was having an early Monday morning breakfast with her freshmen dorm suitemates.

"Oh, you won't believe *this* one," Bess answered in a tired voice. Her face was smeared with dirt, and her blond hair was tangled with leaves and mud.

"It looks like someone dragged you out of bed in the middle of the night and made you run an obstacle course," Eileen's roommate, Reva Ross, said as she tried unsuccessfully to suppress a smile. "What's going on?"

Bess and Eileen looked at each other and sighed.

"Someone dragged us out of bed in the middle of the night ..." Bess began wearily.

"But I don't remember hearing anything last night," Reva interrupted, speaking to Eileen. "I woke up this morning, and your bed was empty."

"That's because they didn't really *drag* us out of bed," Eileen explained. "They had us meet them in the quad."

"To run an 'errand,' " Bess added. "Which was really a treasure hunt. All over the Wilder University campus. For the last six hours." Bess noticed Nancy staring at her in disbelief. "Yes, *another* stupid Kappa pledge stunt," she said to Nancy, laughing good-naturedly. "So come on, go ahead and get the snickering over with."

"Don't tell me these sorority stunts are finally getting to you," Casey Fontaine, another of Nancy's suitemates, said. "You've been really into it so far."

"Yeah, and luckily you've been around to witness all of my humiliations," Bess commented. She eyed Nancy's chocolate-chip pancakes.

"Suddenly I'm starved, and those look great," she said. "Come on, Eileen, I'd say we've earned a break."

Bess pulled over an empty chair from another table and squeezed in next to Nancy. Her wet clothes squished as she settled in the chair.

"You don't regret pledging, do you?" Nancy

asked, moving away as Bess's clothes started dripping on her.

"No way!" Bess said, snatching Nancy's plate of untouched pancakes.

"I mean, all this stuff is pretty fun. It's only when I'm exhausted and hungry, like now, that it's hard to remember exactly why I wanted to join."

"Are these people you really want to be friends with?" Reva marveled.

"They *do* put you through the wringer," Nancy added.

"They're a little hard on the pledge pranks," Eileen agreed. "But that's all part of it." She sat down between Reva and another of her suite-mates, Ginny Yuen.

"It's almost as bad for them as it is for us. I mean, *they* had to get up in the middle of the night to meet us," Eileen said as she dug into a bowl of cereal.

Nancy glanced at the muddy puddle forming under Bess's feet. "It kind of looks like they sent you out into the jungle," she said.

Bess waved her comment off. "What's a little walk in the woods?" she said with a shrug. "It wasn't too bad."

"Except for the sleep deprivation," Ginny reminded her.

"I heard they make the guys pledging frats do some really ridiculous stuff," Reva added. "Like blindfolding them and dropping them off in the middle of the next state—without any clothes."

There was a long second of silence, then the table erupted in howling laughter.

"I have to admit," Ginny said, dabbing her eyes, "it's a pretty funny picture."

"Not so loud," Eileen said. "You might give someone ideas."

"Speaking of ideas," Reva cut in. "I believe that before we were interrupted by our muddy pledges, we were on the subject of Ginny's lyric ideas for Ray's song."

Reva was referring to Ginny's boyfriend, Ray Johannson, a Wilder student and the lead singer of an alternative-music band called the Beat Poets. Ginny had written lyrics for one of Ray's songs and had been telling them to her suitemates.

Ginny and Ray were the last people Nancy would have picked to fall in love. He was a little wild, with an earring and a tattoo, and she was bookish and conservative looking.

But that'll teach you to jump to conclusions, Nancy chided herself. They may be the most oddly matched couple on campus, but they're also one of the tightest.

Nancy fanned her face with her napkin. "Pretty nice, having a sexy rock singer for a boyfriend," she said, and sighed.

Ginny stuck her tongue out at her suitemate.

"If I didn't know better, I'd say you were jealous."

"Well, if she's not jealous, can *I* be?" Casey Fontaine threw in.

Reva rolled her eyes in mock indignation. "What are *you* complaining about, Fontaine? Not only are you tall and gorgeous, and the star of your own TV show, and, and, um—wait I'll get it—"

"You also have your own too-sexy boyfriend!" Nancy helped out.

Reva nodded at Nancy. "Right, Charley Stern," she declared. "L.A. cutie-pie."

Charley, featured regularly in supermarket tabloids and glossy pictorials, had been Casey's costar on the TV sitcom *The President's Daughter*. Casey had been the star of the show before she decided to go to college.

Casey picked a cereal *O* out of Eileen's bowl, and held it up to the light, pretending to study it carefully. "He's okay, I guess," she said with feigned boredom.

"Casey, if you're tired of him, I'll take him off your hands," Nancy teased.

Casey gave Nancy a satisfied smile. "In your dreams."

"You sure you don't need any help?" George Fayne called out to Will Blackfeather from the steps of his apartment house. The echoes of the Wilder clock tower chiming ten o'clock wafted through the neighborhood of Victorian houses just off campus.

In her jeans, baggy fleece jacket, red hat, and big, clunky hiking boots, George combed her fingers through her thick brown curls and brushed at the dust. She and Will were just returning from three days of camping in the woods, a day more than they'd planned.

Will shook his head no at her, smiling, and leaned into the back of his car for the rest of the camping gear. He was wearing jeans, a jacket over a flannel shirt, and heavy hiking boots. George couldn't help but notice how muscular he was. She knew he was beautiful the second she laid eyes on him across a sea of heads in the dining hall her first dinner on campus. But she didn't know how beautiful. Not until this weekend.

I can't believe he's all mine, she mused, struggling to keep herself from laughing out loud.

As Will strode up the walk toward her, his arms full, they exchanged broad smiles. "I—" he began to say, but didn't finish. He didn't need to. His big, brown eyes said it all. I love you.

"I love you, too," George whispered. Leaning her head against Will's muscular chest, she listened to his beating heart. The thumping was like music. Everything about him was special now. Everything was different—Will, school, her life. Nothing would be the same again.

As if he'd read her mind, Will let out a little

laugh of pleasure. "This weekend was the best time of my life," he said lovingly.

"Mine, too," George said, sure now that her decision to take the "final step" in her relationship with Will had been the right one.

Their first night at the campsite, they kissed until they fell asleep in each other's arms. But the second night, they both felt the time had come. The moon was streaking through the clouds, showering their campsite with white moonlight. The night air was surprisingly warm, and the only sounds were the crickets chirping softly in the trees and the nearby brook gurgling against the rocks. Will had held her gently as they stretched out side by side in their tent, which they'd set up on a springy bed of pine needles.

Surprisingly, George hadn't felt uncomfortable. Will was gentle and loving—and he'd thought of everything. She didn't even have to bring up the subject of protection. They'd talked it all out before.

The next morning the sun nudged them awake through the screen door with warm light. The first thing George saw were Will's smiling eyes peering into hers. "Hi, beautiful," he'd said, and she melted again into his arms.

"Hey, George!" a voice cried, snapping George out of her reverie. "We missed you at crew practice this morning!"

George looked up to catch one of her teammates flying by on her bicycle.

"You're not mad you missed practice, are you?" Will asked.

George smiled ironically. "I'm sure the coach'll let me make it up with some extra wind sprints tomorrow. But I will have to get the notes from my nine o'clock calculus class. The professor loves to give pop quizzes."

George helped Will inside with the stuff. As they walked up the stairs, they were quiet. George didn't feel giddy—she felt romantic, in love, and calm.

Then she thought of her friends, Nancy and Bess. I want them to know, George decided. But know what? How much should she tell them?

Telling Nancy would be easier. George had told her about her plans with Will. But George felt a pang of guilt when it came to Bess. She didn't purposely *not* tell her. It just hadn't come up. They'd both been so busy, George hadn't found a chance to talk to Bess. Now Bess was going to find out after the fact. She'd better try to see Nancy and Bess as soon as possible. Maybe they could have lunch today.

"Shoot," George murmured as she followed Will into his apartment.

"What is it?" he asked, reading her expression.

George pecked him on the cheek. "Nothing," she said. But telling Bess wasn't nothing. She didn't want this to put a damper on a momentous weekend. But she knew it had potential for disappointment.

*   *   *

"Ugh," Liz Bader groaned. "This is *hard.*"

"You're telling me," chimed in a voice from the other side of the flimsy partition.

Curling stray strands of her short auburn bob behind her ears, Liz raised her eyes to her early attempts at architectural drawing that she'd pinned to the partition and grimaced. The chest-high partitions divided the massive architecture studio in Rand Hall into a crazy maze of individual spaces—which did help Liz concentrate, but also helped her get lost every time she left her own drafting table. Even after a few weeks, it still took her a couple laps around the studio to find her cubicle again.

"Are you getting any work done, Jenny?" Liz called out to the voice on the other side of the partition.

"Working would be generous. More like flailing."

Liz rolled her eyes with relief. At least I'm not the only one.

"Let's take a break and go downstairs. Maybe some coffee will juice us up."

Jenny poked her white-blond head around the corner and sighed. "I don't know how I'm going to get this done on time."

Liz smiled at her. "Jenny, your lips are blue."

"I know," Jenny groaned, and rubbed her sleeve across her mouth. "All the pens leak."

"Well, at least stop biting your fingernails."

"I can't," Jenny said. "I'm nervous. I don't think I'm going to finish my project before we have to pin up."

Pinning up was what the students had to do at the end of a project. All their drawings went up on a wall in one of the big empty rooms downstairs, and then the professors critiqued their work. Liz and her studiomates had been through it twice already, and it was unbelievably nerve-racking and only a little kinder than what the Spanish Inquisition sounded like. So far, though, they'd only been doing little projects and exercises. They were supposed to get their first big assignment soon.

"Are you two taking a break?" another voice called out.

"Are you eavesdropping?" Jenny shot back.

"Just looking for a reason to stop working," the voice replied. "Hey, Studio One, break time in the Cave!"

Liz laughed as she listened to the sound of stools scraping back and the moaning and groaning of the other kids in her studio. She looked at Jenny and shrugged.

"It's always nice to have company when you procrastinate."

"Yeah," Jenny agreed. "I won't feel guilty that everyone else is working harder than me."

Downstairs in the Cave, the cafeteria under Rand Hall, a group of six freshmen architects dragged benches and chairs over to a huge slate table. A couple of sophomores sat slumped over their coffees with circles under their eyes. Liz's gaze wandered around the grungy little snack-eteria. It was almost always filled with architecture students. So far, she hadn't experienced an all-nighter, but she was staying in the studio later and later. And the later it got, the more upperclassmen came out of the woodwork. After sophomore year, she'd been told, she'd practically live in the studio.

It still made her laugh to notice the empty soda cans glued to the ceiling by the students who decorated the Cave. Paintings of colorful dragons and futuristic buildings wrapped around the walls. The whole scene, with all the artsy stuff on the walls and all the funky people hanging out, was exactly what Liz had dreamed of when she'd applied to Wilder for architecture.

It's weird, but it's perfect! she thought happily.

"Have you guys gotten your first big assignment yet?" one of the second-year students asked.

"You've *got* to be kidding," Jenny replied.

"Yeah, she's just getting the hang of holding the pens," Liz quipped, giving Jenny a friendly wink.

"Well, don't get too attached to your bed," another sophomore advised with a sleepy nod.

"And you can say goodbye to your social life," a guy said as he plopped down in the empty chair next to Liz's. Liz couldn't take her eyes off him.

That was how it had been when she first met him last night.

He was very cute, with short black hair, and electric green eyes behind round wire-rimmed glasses. Liz couldn't help admiring his clothes—he seemed to be a fan of her favorite color—black T-shirt, black jeans, and black shoes. He was the closest thing to New York City Liz had seen in weeks, and that alone made her grin. Immediately, he smiled back.

"Daniel Frederick," he said, introducing himself to Jenny. "Hi, again," he said to Liz.

"This is Jenny Osborne," Liz replied, nodding toward her friend. "And speaking of social life, I was already getting the feeling that I'd never see my suitemates again."

Daniel shrugged, unimpressed.

"But you don't come to college to hang out in your room," Liz quickly added.

"Brace yourself," Daniel warned. "You haven't seen anything yet. The architecture professors give you about a month to settle in, then whammo! It'll be like you're quarantined here in Rand Hall. The only people you'll ever see again are your studiomates."

And what would be wrong with that? Liz thought dreamily, eyeing Daniel.

"What studio are you in?" Jenny inquired.

Daniel directed his answer to Liz. "Yours," he replied with a grin, as he got up to go. He turned to Jenny. "First- and second-year students share the first floor. I'm sure we'll run into each other again." He stared pointedly at Liz. "I'll see you later, okay?"

Liz nodded happily as Daniel and a couple of the other second-year students finished their coffee, then took off down the tunnel for the stairs.

Liz felt a sudden surge of brain power. Maybe it was the coffee. Or maybe it was something else ... "Well, back to the salt mines," she said cheerfully, pushing away from the table.

"Where's the fire?" Jenny replied sluggishly.

"Oh, nowhere." Liz smiled. Inwardly, the thought was burning in her mind: being quarantined in Rand Hall wouldn't be bad at all, if she was with Daniel Frederick.

CHAPTER 2

Pepperoni or triple olive and sausage?" Ray Johansson asked Ginny as he peered into the pizza box.

"I want *you*," Ginny said to her rocker boyfriend. "With extra cheese."

"Gross!" Spider cried.

Ginny and Ray were with Spider and Bruce, two members of Ray's band, the Beat Poets. Everyone was sitting on milk crates in Spider's garage on the outskirts of the Wilder campus. It was lunchtime during one of the band's marathon practice sessions, and Ginny had brought over a stack of pizzas. "You think these pies'll last until dinner?"

"Maybe afternoon tea," Bruce replied, his mouth already full.

Ray rolled his eyes. "You two are slobs."

"Who cares? They can play!" Ginny said.

Spider held up two fists, each clenched around a slice of pizza. "Right on!"

"So did you tell her, Ray?" Bruce asked excitedly.

Ginny looked at Ray, mesmerized. *I still can't believe he loves me,* she thought.

Until recently, she'd feared that she wasn't cool enough to have Ray for a boyfriend. Sexy singers didn't go out with nerdy premeds like her.

But as different as they were, she knew that inside they were soulmates. She felt it. And, the best part was, so did he.

"Tell me what?" she asked.

"Oh, nothing—" Ray said, staring down at his feet.

Ginny could feel something was up. "Tell me *what?*" she complained.

"Remember what I promised you about our song?" Ray began, his voice steady and cool.

Ginny nodded eagerly. *How could she forget?* The song was called "Trust." It was the song she had told her suitemates about at breakfast. He'd written the music, and she'd written the lyrics. She'd never tried writing a song before, but with Ray as inspiration, anything seemed possible. When the Beat Poets debuted it the week before at a campus nightclub, the Underground, the crowd went wild. It was a hit!

"Ray." Ginny tugged eagerly at his sleeve.

"I did something behind your back," Ray continued sheepishly. "Spider, Bruce, and I recorded a demo of it and sent it around to a few record companies . . ."

Ray stopped and casually took a bite of pizza. Ginny thought she was going to explode with anticipation.

"Ray!" she shrieked again.

"So, one of them liked it," Ray said nonchalantly.

Ginny held her breath. "You're kidding," she whispered. "Right?"

Spider shook his stringy blond hair. Bruce smiled his gap-toothed smile. "Nope," they said in unison.

"They're really interested in our sound and want to talk about working together," Ray said calmly. "But that's not the best part. The best part is that their favorite thing about the song was the lyrics."

Ginny couldn't tell if this was a joke or not. She knew Spider, Bruce, and Ray constantly played elaborate practical jokes on one another.

Ginny waved them off. "Very funny. Ha, ha."

Ray shrugged. "She doesn't believe us, guys."

Rolling his eyes, Spider fished deep in his front pocket and offered up a piece of paper folded in eights.

Ginny unfolded it slowly. "Oh wow!" Ginny yelled as she read the letter. The letterhead belonged to an executive from Pacific Records. The

Beat Poets weren't a pipe dream anymore. They were for real!

Ginny smoothed the paper out on her leg, then grabbed Ray around the neck and planted a kiss on his lips.

Spider and Bruce laughed and pretended to hide their eyes. "Hey! Come on!"

But Ginny was so excited, she kissed them all in turn. "This is awesome. I can't wait to tell Liz!"

"Yeah, if you ever see her again," Ray said.

"True," Ginny said, remembering that the last time she'd seen her roommate was three days ago, heading toward Rand Hall with an armful of architectural drawing supplies.

Ginny hopped to her feet. "Well, back to work," she commanded, kicking the pizza boxes closed. "Practice, practice, practice! There's no time to waste."

"Where are you going?" Ray called after her.

"Where else? To tell all my friends!"

"Hey, our letter!" Spider complained.

Ginny waved it in the air. "I'm going to have it framed!" She sprinted into the warm afternoon sun.

"Hey, guys," Nancy said as she slid into a booth opposite Bess and George at the Souvlaki House, a popular greasy-spoon diner on the edge of campus. "Sorry I'm late."

"No problem," Bess said. "I was just catching

George up on play rehearsal gossip. It feels like I haven't seen you guys in ages." She looked up at Nancy. "Well, George, that is. I just saw you at breakfast." Bess rolled her eyes and grimaced.

"George, lunch was such a good idea. I'm glad we could all make it on such short notice. *So*," Nancy said, leaning across the table toward George. "How was your trip?"

George blushed and grinned. "It was really great, Nan," she said meaningfully.

Bess's eyes widened. "I forgot! You went camping!"

Nancy grinned at George. "So?"

Bess knotted her brow. "What's the big deal? George goes camping all the time. Ugh, sleeping with all those bugs. Thanks but no thanks."

Nancy looked at Bess. Sleeping with bugs? Bess's face didn't show any anticipation or surprise. Nancy glanced quickly at George, who was gazing at her plate, and realized that George hadn't told Bess what she'd planned to do with Will. Nancy was surprised. George usually told Bess everything.

Nancy kicked George under the table.

George shrugged. "I didn't have a chance—"

"To what?" Bess asked.

"To tell you," George said. "About the weekend."

"But I know," Bess replied cheerfully. "Camping in the woods."

18

"You know?" George asked. "But how could you know?"

Bess laughed. "But you *told* me." Bess stopped, obviously confused. "Didn't you?"

Nancy breathed a sigh of relief as the waitress came to take their orders. "I'll have a pita burger."

"Me, too," George said.

"Make it three," Bess said, then turned her attention to George. "Is there something you're keeping from me. George? I mean, you *did* go camping, right?"

George nodded. "But it was more than that. We . . . um. Will and I . . . we're really happy, and—"

Bess feigned shock. "You got married!" she joked.

Nancy and George laughed nervously. "No, no, of course not."

Abruptly, Bess narrowed her eyes. "Did you and Will . . ." she said, and Nancy knew she'd figured it out.

George nodded. "Yes," she said simply.

Instead of bubbling over with excitement, as Nancy knew Bess normally would, she merely smiled. "Oh. So . . . why didn't you tell me?" she asked, obviously hurt.

"I didn't have a chance—" she started to say.

"But you told Nancy," Bess said.

Nancy reached across and pressed Bess's hand. "Bess, don't you remember? Last week you were either in rehearsal or at the Kappa house every single night. . . ."

Bess slowly withdrew her hand. "I'm really happy for you, George," she said.

Nancy could see that Bess's reactions were now upsetting George. But Nancy thought George shouldn't be. This was such a happy time in her life.

George finally nudged Bess. "Come on," she said. "Let's go outside for a second. You don't mind, do you, Nan?"

Nancy shook her head. "I'm hungry enough for three pita burgers, anyway."

George and Bess went outside. When the sandwiches came, Nancy sighed at all the food. She shook out some ketchup next to her home fries and started to dig in. She was just finishing up her plate when Will slid into the booth opposite her.

"Hungry?" he asked, eyeing the two full platters.

"George and Bess are outside."

Will nodded. "They're sitting on a bench across the street. They looked like they were having a real heart-to-heart, so I didn't think I should interfere."

Nancy smiled. She didn't know Will very well. She liked him because George cared about him. But at that moment, she went from merely liking him to liking him a lot. She knew that a lot of guys wouldn't have understood why it was important for George to spend this time with Bess.

"I'm really happy for you guys," Nancy said.

Will blushed. "Thanks," he said. "That means a lot. You and Bess are everything to George."

"Not everything." Nancy smiled. "Not anymore."

The color of Will's face deepened. "So she told you."

Nancy sighed. "I guess we'll be spending a lot more time together," she said, faking disappointment.

"I hope so," Will replied.

"Stop right there!" George cried as she strode through the door. "Don't touch that burger!"

"Or that one!" Bess echoed, close on George's heels.

As George and Bess slid back into their seats, Bess seemed to be a little happier, but Nancy could tell she wasn't totally satisfied.

"One big happy family again?" Will asked the table.

Bess smiled weakly. "One big happy family," she replied quietly.

"Concentrate!" Brian Daglian shouted at Bess two hours later. "Project! Sing from your diaphragm!"

Bess was standing onstage in the theater arts building. Brian was sitting in the fifth row with his feet kicked up on the seat in front of him. They'd been taking turns rehearsing their chorus parts in the musical *Grease!* for over an hour.

21

Bess thought her voice sounded as beautiful as hissing steam that day.

She raised her arms, lifted her chin, and gave it one more shot. But her notes took a nosedive and sounded like the call of a floundering duck.

She gave up and sat heavily on the edge of the stage. Brian hopped up beside her, and Bess leaned against his shoulder.

"Emotion check," he said. "What's up?"

"I don't have any friends," Bess muttered. Brian cleared his throat. "Except you, of course," she added quickly.

"Okay, what did Nancy and George do *this* time?" Brian asked, rolling his eyes.

Bess laughed. "Am I that obvious?"

"Bess, you're an open book. That's one of things I love about you."

Bess looked at Brian, and for a second she experienced another of her occasional flashes of regret that he'd never be more than a friend. When Bess first met him at class registration, she was wild about him. He was gorgeous—blond, blue-eyed, and very funny. Then he told her he was gay, and their friendship grew, especially with Nancy so busy at the newspaper, and George spending more and more time with Will—

Which was exactly the problem.

"George kept something from me, something really huge, and I'm really bummed."

Brian nodded decisively. "She definitely hates you."

22

Bess gave him a playful slap. "It's not funny!"

"Okay—did she keep it secret on purpose?" Brian asked.

Bess shrugged. "Well—she told Nancy."

"Are you sure she just hadn't gotten around to telling you yet?"

"If it were anything else, maybe," Bess replied. "But not this."

Brian leaned forward. "You've got me interested now. What's the big secret?"

Bess shrugged, trying to play it off as unimportant. "George and Will started sleeping together."

Brian nodded. "Yeah?"

"Well. It's just that—that I can't believe George didn't tell me what she was planning, too. We're cousins and have been best friends *forever*. Now I guess she's only talking to Nancy."

Brian looked her in the eye. "You're not just jealous of George's relationship, are you?"

Bess hadn't thought of that. She didn't think she was.

"I'm incredibly happy for George and Will," she said firmly. "That's not the point. I just want to be able to continue to tell them about *my* stuff, too. Like, if there was something huge in my life, I'd want to talk to them about it. But if we're keeping secrets, I don't know."

There was a long pause, and Bess thought Brian was thinking over what she'd said. When she looked at him, though, he was staring off into space. "Uh, Brian?"

"Sorry," Brian said, startled. "What were you saying?"

"Nothing important," Bess said. She gave him a sidelong glance. "Are *you* okay?"

Brian smiled tightly. "Great! Everything's great!" he said a little too quickly.

"Uh-huh," Bess said. "I really believe you, too."

Come to think of it, Bess thought, Brian had seemed distracted lately. During his most important scene the night before, he actually missed a cue. Normally Brian was one of the most dependable members of the cast.

"How's Chris?" Bess asked, wondering if Brian's distraction had anything to do with Chris Vogel, the guy he was seeing. "Have you talked any more about—you know, talking to your parents about your lifestyle? Forget it," she said quickly. "It's none of my business."

Brian sighed and stretched out on the empty stage. "No, it's okay. To tell you the truth, it has been on my mind—night and day. Chris has been very patient and understanding."

"So, what about your parents?" Bess probed.

Brian was quiet a moment before he spoke. "My mom will be totally cool about it. She's cool about everything. In fact, I think she already knows. She senses things. You know what I mean?"

24

Bess nodded and smiled. "My mother always knows what's going on in my life without my telling her," she said. She looked meaningfully at Brian. "Is it your dad?"

"Actually," Brian said, sitting up and staring Bess in the face. "It's not my dad I'm worried about, either."

"Whoa!" Nancy yelled. "Hey, Kara, watch where you're throwing that stuff!"

Kara Verbeck glanced over her shoulder. Her shoe had just whistled past Nancy's ear, ricocheted off the wall, and dropped onto her desk, where she was reading.

"Sorry." Kara shrugged and turned back to her closet. Wearing nothing but underwear, she ran her fingers through her long brown hair. There was nothing left in her closet but empty hangers. "Oh, I just can't find *anything* to wear."

Nancy peered over the top of her Western civ textbook. "I guess the three dozen shirts and twenty skirts and ten pairs of pants you've shoveled out of there don't qualify," she quipped. "Not to mention the small mountain of clothes, which looked suspiciously like mine, that I found piled at the foot of my bed."

Kara blew a strand of hair out of her eyes and flapped her arms. "It's useless. Everything I own is worthless!"

"Aren't you going to a lot of trouble to look good to study for your psychology test?"

Kara waved her hand. "Oh, that . . . Yeah, I'm going to study. But I have to look good because it's not *what* I'm going to study. It's *who* I'm going to study *with*. Liz introduced me to a guy last night. He's a friend of Liz's, or a friend of a friend—something like that. His name is Tim—I think. But he *is* definitely cool. Or at least that's what Liz says. And *cute*."

Nancy tilted her head. "Really. What a surprise."

Kara hopped to her feet. "This room is exhausted territory," she declared, marching out of the room and across the hall, still in her underwear. She walked through Liz and Ginny's door without knocking. Ginny was bent over her desk, staring into her computer and mumbling to herself.

"Knock, knock," Kara said, and bounced over to Liz's closet and started fingering through it.

"Uh, can I help you?" Ginny asked.

"No, that's okay. I'm just browsing . . . Ugh, *nothing!*"

Ginny came over to help. "You've got to be kidding. Liz has *great* clothes."

"But everything's black! And black isn't my color."

"I might have something," Ginny said, leading Kara over to her dresser. She started pulling things out and laying them on the bed. Kara shook her head and hid her eyes.

"Thanks, Gin," she said politely. "But—"

Ginny shrugged. "Okay, so I don't have the most dynamic wardrobe in the world. Where are you going, anyway?"

Kara waved a hand in the air as though it were irrelevant. "Oh, just on a date with some guy Liz introduced me to."

"You mean you've actually *seen* Liz?"

Kara nodded. "Sure. Haven't you?"

"She's so busy she comes in after I'm asleep and leaves before I wake up. I feel like I live in a single," Ginny said.

"A single? Cool!"

Ginny shrugged. "Yeah, I guess. Though sometimes, when I come back from class, it would be nice to have a roommate to talk to again."

When Kara returned to her room, she saw Nancy had laid out a clingy black sheath, a black leather jacket, and a pair of dangly stone earrings.

"Excellent!" Kara cooed. "Are these for me?"

Nancy laughed. "They're for *me*. But tonight, you can *wear* them."

Kara nodded with approval, then something struck her and she narrowed her eyes at Nancy. "Where have you been hiding this stuff?"

"That's for me to know and for you *not* to find out!" Nancy threw on an oversize Wilder sweatshirt, heaved her book bag over one shoulder, and headed for the door. "Besides," she called behind her. "I have a study date, too."

"You have a date?" Kara asked, amazed.

Nancy laughed. "Aren't I allowed?"

"Sure, but look what you're wearing!"

"Well, *my* date's a little less glamorous. It's with a really cute—library. Have fun!" Nancy said, and twirled out of the room.

Standing in front of the mirror, holding up the clingy dress with one hand and the earrings with the other, Kara gazed approvingly at her reflection. "Oh, I will," she murmured.

CHAPTER 3

Nancy was staring out the big third-floor window next to her study carrel. Across the quad, the sun was setting behind the clock tower, and the sky was smoldering with all the colors of the rainbow. The Wilder campus below her was glowing with the last light of day.

Nancy was having a hard time keeping her mind on studying. The view was a lot more interesting. Even though she'd only been in the library for three hours or so, it felt as if she'd been there for days.

I'm not getting much accomplished, she thought dryly.

Nancy glared at the pile of note cards in front of her. Okay—ready, set, organize!

Somehow, the mass of thoughts and literary criticism had to transform itself into a five-page paper on William Faulkner by Wednesday afternoon, and it was Monday night already.

What she was doing instead of writing was thinking about George and Will and their decision. Ever since George had told her about her and Will's plan to take their big step together, Nancy had started wondering about *her* first time. For years and years she'd assumed it would be with her old boyfriend, Ned Nickerson. So did everyone else, though no one actually said so.

"So maybe he wasn't the right guy," she murmured pensively as she studied her reflection in the window. "Maybe I was fooling myself."

One thing was for sure—it wasn't the kind of thing she could rush. It was too important. Now that she and Ned weren't together anymore, she was on her own.

"No," Nancy mused out loud. "It's not going to be with just anybody."

Then Peter Goodwin's face popped to the front of her mind. "It might have been you," Nancy said quietly.

Peter was a junior who had lived on the floor below her suite until the week before. Their attraction had been undeniable.

But their relationship had been doomed from the start. Peter had harbored an enormous secret: he had a child with an ex-girlfriend from high school. And by the time he confessed how attracted he was to Nancy, his guilt about being away from his son and his fear of getting involved with someone new caused him to cut their relationship off before it could become anything serious. He moved out of Thayer to a single in another dorm across campus, and now he went home most weekends to see his son.

Nancy's eyes rose to the other side of campus. She could see his dorm. Most of the windows were lit up. "Which one's yours?" she wondered out loud. Although you only live across campus, I feel you're out of my life—for good."

Footsteps yanked Nancy out of her thoughts. She heard giggly laughter and a deep sigh. It was a couple, strangers, walking by arm in arm, their book bags slung over their shoulders, oblivious to the world.

Nancy smiled at them cheerlessly, as she remembered that her father was coming up on Thursday with his new girlfriend, Avery. Her father had gone on an occasional date since her mother had died when Nancy was three. But Nancy had never thought of any of them as a replacement for her mother. Not until now. There had been something in her father's voice, something he wasn't saying, that made Nancy think he was already in love with Avery.

Everyone's in love, Nancy lamented. Except me.

Nancy stood and stretched. She left her carrel, going nowhere in particular. She did a lap around the third floor, observing all the local life—students drooling onto their notebooks, dead asleep;

others whispering with their boyfriends or girl-friends. One or two study grinds scribbled furiously in notebooks or tapped away at their laptop computers. Nancy bought a can of soda and a candy bar at one of the vending machines outside the study room on the second floor and leaned against the wall, munching away.

Out of the corner of her eye, she noticed some sharp movement in the far corner of the study room. A cute guy in a faded denim jacket was checking right and left, as if to see that the coast was clear. Then, after opening a red gym bag, he grabbed a desktop globe and shoved it in his bag. Then he pulled a note from his pocket and put it where the globe had been. Just as he swung the bag onto his shoulder, he noticed Nancy in the doorway.

Nancy stood her ground. They eyed each other for a second. Then the guy gave her an uncomfortable shrug and strode to the opposite side of the study room, ducking through a door there.

Nancy stepped inside and went over to the table. She picked up the note. "Of the entire world, only a few ..."

Shaking her head, Nancy scanned the room. No one else seemed to have noticed the young man take the globe. "Why am I always in the wrong place at the right time?" she wondered out loud.

She glanced at the note again. That's weird. Why would he leave a note? she asked herself.

Walking out of the study room toward the librarian's desk, Nancy wasn't sure whether or not to report the theft. The globe *was* school property. Then again, the note made it seem more like a prank. She tried to remember what the guy looked like.

"Nancy," someone called in a loud whisper.

Nancy whipped around. Liz Bader was walking toward her. She got halfway across the floor, stopped and turned back, and beckoned to somebody in the doorway. When he stepped out, he was smoothing his hair. Nancy almost laughed out loud. The guy was practically a replica of Liz, dressed in black from neck to toe. He even walked with the same swagger. He's probably from New York City, too, Nancy thought.

"Nancy," Liz said excitedly. "I *have* to talk to you."

"Nancy, this is Daniel Frederick. Daniel—Nancy Drew," Liz said, ushering them both into the library lounge.

"Let me guess," Nancy said to Daniel. "You're an architecture major, too, right?"

"How did you know?" Liz asked, surprised by Nancy's comment.

"You have that up-all-night look," Nancy joked. "Just like Liz."

Liz blushed. "I didn't realize we looked that tired," she said, and smiled, glancing over at Daniel.

As she took him in, Liz thought that she couldn't be happier. She knew that when she got to college, she'd start making friends, but she couldn't have imagined what a close-knit bunch of people the architecture students were. Something about spending day after day in the studio together bonded everyone in the program, like a family.

"Hey, guys," someone said, coming into the lounge.

"Tim!" Liz said, recognizing the cute guy in the faded denim jacket.

Tim Downing was a pledge in Daniel's fraternity, Alpha Delta. When Tim had stopped by to see Daniel the night before, Daniel had introduced him to Liz and they'd hit it off instantly. She thought he was cute, with his longish brown hair. He also had an upbeat personality, which was why Liz had introduced him to Kara.

"I was just about to rescue you both for a coffee break," Tim said with a big grin.

"Yeah, a commando raid," Daniel kidded. "With ropes and guns and everything."

Liz was about to introduce Nancy to Tim when she noticed that Tim's smile faded when he saw Nancy. Now he was examining his shoelaces hard. Liz couldn't figure out why.

"Uh, this is Tim Downing," Liz said uncertainly.

"Where's your red gym bag?" Nancy interrupted, smiling strangely.

Red gym bag? What is she talking about? Liz wondered. "You know Tim, Nance?"

"Not really," Nancy said meaningfully—as if she really did.

Now everyone was staring at Tim, who was looking at the ceiling, as if casting around in his brain for something to say.

Liz laughed. "Tim, I didn't realize you were so shy. Tim is rushing Daniel's fraternity, and according to Daniel, he's incredibly talkative," she explained.

"I think my roommate, Kara Verbeck, was just speaking about you," Nancy said. "Didn't you two have a study date tonight?"

Tim's face broke into a smile.

"Yeah, I wonder how much studying you actually got done." Daniel laughed.

"So *you're* Kara's roommate," Tim said, his smile fading.

Nancy nodded. "Small *world*, isn't it?"

There was another uncomfortable pause before Tim said, "Wow, look at the time, I gotta go! I have—some work to do."

Before Liz or Daniel could ask him to stay, Tim had walked away.

Liz scratched her head. "He sure was acting strange," she said to Daniel. Before he could reply, a voice called out from the doorway.

"Yeah, you guys look like you're going to a funeral." A husky, blond young man came clumping into the lounge.

"Hey, Chipper!" Daniel said, shaking the guy's hand. "Everyone, this is Chip Booth. Chip—Liz Bader, and—and—"

"Nancy Drew," Liz interceded.

"Sorry," Daniel apologized. "I've had so much work to do, my mind's like a sieve. The other night I was walking home, and I forgot which frat house I lived in!"

Chip clapped Daniel on the shoulder. "Do you mean you forgot you're a member of Alpha Delt?" He asked with mock severity.

"I like your bag," Nancy said, eyeing the red gym bag dangling from Chip's shoulder.

Liz threw Nancy an uncomprehending look. "What *is* it with these bags, Nan?"

"Good question," Nancy said. "Maybe Chip can enlighten us. Is carrying a red gym bag part of the Alpha Delt brotherhood or something? That one looks a lot like the one Tim Downing had."

Chip laughed. "Everyone in the house has one."

Daniel smiled tightly. "It's a secret sign," he said spookily, wriggling his fingers in front of his face. "If you look at it too closely, it'll burn your eyes out."

"Daniel!" Liz scolded him. "Don't be dumb."

Daniel shrugged.

"Hey, bro," Chip said, steering Daniel away by the shoulder. "We have house business. Sorry, girls, but we've got to run."

"Sometimes this frat stuff seems so *bizarre.*" Liz said as she watched the guys leave the lounge. She turned and noticed Nancy watching the closing door with a strange expression on her face.

"You're telling me," Nancy replied thoughtfully.

"So are you going to invite me in, or what?" Chris asked hesitantly.

Brian sighed and leaned back against a tree, his clear blue eyes blinking in the streetlight. He and Chris were standing outside his dorm. He'd just blown off all his work to have pizza. He should have been studying. Or working on the play. Or reading. Or doing something. Not eating pizza with Chris, spending time with him when he could have been doing, what?

"I kind of have to study," he said unconvincingly.

Chris held Brian's gaze. "You kind of have to study?" he said incredulously. "You didn't kind of have to study an hour ago. What's the emergency?"

Brian shrugged.

"Why don't you tell me what's really bothering you?" Chris asked firmly.

Brian forced himself to smile. "Nothing," he said. "I had a great time. It's just that, that I—"

"I know, I know," Chris cut him off. "You have to study."

Brian smiled at Chris. He *did* like him. When he was alone in his room—he was one of the few freshmen lucky to have a single—and he closed his eyes against the rest of the world, forgetting what everyone else would think, he thought about how lucky he was to have Chris for a friend.

So what's the problem? he challenged himself. Why don't you invite him upstairs to hang out?

"Because I can't," he answered himself out loud.

Chris peered at him. "Because you can't what?"

Brian reddened. "Was I talking to myself again?"

"Are you sure you're okay?" Chris asked, concerned.

Brian just stared. Chris was standing in front of him, but all Brian could see was the message that he had found scrawled in weird zigzags on a piece of paper under his door.

What's your secret? I know. And soon so will the rest of the world. Even your father. Bye-bye—for now. We'll chat soon.

"Okay." Chris sighed resignedly. "I know there's something you're not telling me. But I can see I won't be able to convince you to talk about it."

All I want to do *is* tell you! Brian screamed

in his mind. But knowing you, you'd want to take action and find out who wrote the note. But if you *really* knew me, you'd know that I'm the kind of guy who doesn't like to make waves.

"Chris, I'm sorry," Brian said, and he meant it.

"Can I call you tomorrow?" Chris asked.

Brian smiled. "You can even call me later tonight."

Brian watched Chris go until he was swallowed up by the darkness, then turned and walked into his own dorm. He took the stairs slowly, thinking about his homework and also about all the things he was discovering about himself. By the time he reached his door, his mind was swimming: half with hopes and half with fears.

Inside his room he sat on his bed and noticed his answering machine blinking. He leaned back against his pillows and tapped the button to play back the message. He closed his eyes as the tape whirred, then stopped and played.

The second Brian heard the message, his eyes flew open, and he sat bolt upright. This voice wasn't someone he knew. It was low and gravelly, and the tone wasn't friendly. The voice said:

"Daddy has lots of money, and he'd hate to hear about you. What can you do to keep him from knowing? Try borrowing one thousand dollars. And do it soon. Details will follow. Don't ignore me. I'm for real. I'm your worst nightmare. Do what I say—or else."

Brian slammed the answering machine with his fist. He heard the plastic crack and didn't care. He fell back onto the bed and covered his face with his pillow.

CHAPTER 4

Early Tuesday morning Liz was waiting outside the door to the Wilder University Archives when the attendant arrived with his key ring sprouting dozens of keys.

"A little early, aren't you?" the old man said, yawning. "It's not even ten o'clock."

"I need to see the plans for the Alpha Delt fraternity house," Liz explained quickly. "I just got my first assignment—"

The old man held up his hands, as if warding her off. "Don't tell me, don't tell me. 'Wilder on Wilder,' am I right?" he said, reciting the name of Liz's first big assignment for Architecture 1.

Liz nodded. "Very good."

The attendant tapped his temple. "I may be old, but I'm sharp as a whip. In about five minutes there will be a line down the stairs and out

41

the door. Everyone has to pick a building on campus to study."

Liz nodded excitedly. "And I picked the Alpha Delt fraternity house."

The old man nodded admiringly, then leaned forward conspiratorially. "That's my favorite building on campus, too, you know. Especially that funny little building they have on their grounds. What do you call it?"

"The Coop," Liz said. It was the name given to the mysterious circular building that sat about fifty feet from the Alpha Delta house. It was all bricked up and hadn't been used for years, but the fraternity didn't want to tear it down.

"That's it." The old man chuckled to himself. "Always wondered what went on in there in the old days. Anyway, hold on and I'll get you the plans."

As she watched him waddle off, Liz got more and more excited. When she had first received her assignment that morning, she didn't know what building to do. She'd spent so much time in the studio, she hadn't seen much of the campus since she'd been there.

Liz had thought of using her dorm, Thayer Hall, but decided it was boring. The campus clock tower was too obvious, and everyone would probably choose it.

Then it hit her. Daniel's frat house! She wanted to get closer to him, without being too conspicuous. What better way than to study his fraternity house! Besides, the structure was awesome, with its grand columns and huge, wrap-around porch.

"Here you go, Miss," the attendant said, laying the blueprints carefully on the table.

Liz peeled them apart slowly, feeling the thin, paper slip between in her fingers. "These look ancient."

"They're originals," he replied. "More than a hundred years old."

Liz scratched her head. "I'm afraid to work from these."

"Good, because you can't," he replied. "One of the plans is missing, number twelve, I think it is. Anyway, that's what happens when you lend 'em out so much. You make copies from these originals. Just sign here and have them back by the end of the day."

Liz carefully rolled the plans and slid them into the thick tube the attendant had given her. As she left, she felt as if she were carrying top secret plans.

"Let's see—what else do I have to have?" she murmured, thinking about what she'd need to get started. "Coffee!" she remembered—every architect's best friend.

She took the stairs down to the Cave and loaded up for the day: a jumbo coffee, a yogurt for breakfast, and a bagel for lunch. "Um, nutritious," she muttered, and was digging in her pocket for money when a hand appeared out of nowhere and slapped down a few dollar bills. "On the house," a voice said.

"Daniel!" Liz exclaimed, peering up into Daniel's beautiful eyes.

"We have to stop meeting like this," he jested.

Liz tilted her head back and grinned. "Oh, I hope not."

"I'm glad you feel that way," Daniel admitted. "I was wondering if you had plans for Saturday night."

Liz squinted as if racking her brain. "Mmm, let me consult my busy calendar."

"Good," Daniel said with finality. "Because now you do. You're going to let me take you to the Alpha Delt dance."

"I am?" Liz said excitedly. "I mean, I *am!*"

"What's in the tube?" Daniel asked, with a knowing smile. "Wilder on Wilder? So what building did you choose, the clock tower?"

Liz decided it had to be a surprise and only shrugged. Daniel laughed.

"That's okay. Everyone chooses the clock tower," he said. "But I'm not finished inviting you to stuff yet. What are you doing *tomorrow* night?

Liz raised her eyebrows. "Uh, something with you?"

"Bingo!" Daniel replied. "Alpha Delt party. Seven o'clock. Okay? Look, I gotta run. I'm late."

"Me, too," Liz said, following Daniel up to the

studio. It's as if I'm fated to know Alpha Delt, she thought happily. I'm going to know that house better than Daniel could imagine!

Nancy lay on the couch in the suite's lounge, trying to plow through some books of literary criticism for her English paper. She'd be happily concentrating in her room if Kara weren't blabbing on the phone. The books were dry, and Nancy couldn't help nodding off and falling into a light sleep.

The lounge phone suddenly startled her awake. Nancy snatched it before she was ready to talk.

"Hello?" she said groggily.

"Nancy?" the voice said. It was her father, Carson Drew. It was wonderful to hear his deep, throaty voice. He was the one person she could depend on because he was always there for her.

"Dad! I'm so glad you called, but how did you know to call on this phone?"

"Your phone has been busy for the last hour."

Nancy rolled her eyes. "Kara's a one-woman switchboard. She'll call everyone she knows on a whim."

Carson grunted. "I can't wait to meet her," he said unenthusiastically.

"She's quirky but lovable. You'll like her. I do."

"That's good enough for me," he replied. "Look, Nan. I just wanted to firm up our plans. Is Thursday lunch still good for you?"

"Of course," Nancy replied. Though the truth was, no time was good. Not now. Her life was total mayhem, between her friends, her schoolwork, and her assignments for the *Wilder Times*, the school newspaper. And then she had to eat—and sleep.

But on Thursday she'd make time for a long lunch. Her father was bringing Avery Fallon with him to meet Nancy.

"Are you certain?" Carson asked.

"Is anything wrong, Dad?"

There was a long silence. Nancy could hear her father breathing on the other end of the line. She knew him well enough to know he was worried. "Dad?" she repeated.

"I'll be honest with you, Nan," he said. "Avery is very excited to meet you. And you say you're excited to meet her. But personally, I'm very nervous about the whole thing."

"But why? I'm sure we'll get along."

Nancy could practically hear her father sigh with relief. "I hope so," he said. "I really do."

In a strange way Nancy felt better knowing that her father was worried about her meeting Avery. He wasn't taking her for granted, and her opinion was still important to him.

"Actually, Dad," she said. "I have to admit it will be strange to see you in a new relationship. I can tell it's serious and that she's very important to you."

"Does that bother you?" Carson asked point-blank.

Does that bother me? Nancy wondered to herself. I don't know, she concluded. Maybe a little.

"No," she said, cringing. She hated to lie. But it wasn't really a lie. It was just a little fib.

The fact is, Nancy said to him in her mind, I *am* afraid to meet Avery. I'm afraid of losing you . . .

"Besides," she said into the phone. "It's not my decision. It's an adjustment I'll just have to make. All I hope is . . ."

"Yes?" Carson prodded her on.

"That our relationship won't change," Nancy finished, a lump in her throat.

"Never," Carson replied. "Never. Oh, and honey? Remember that computer you said you needed? Well, make sure you clear some room on your desk, because Avery's not the only thing I'm bringing up."

Nancy almost leaped out of her seat. "Dad, really? Excellent!"

When she put the phone down, she thought affectionately of her father.

"I love you, Dad," she murmured.

Stephanie Keats pressed herself against the wall of the hallway and listened to Nancy's conversation.

"I can tell it's serious and that she's very important to you . . ." she overheard Nancy saying.

Stephanie had come out of her room where she'd been primping. The fact was, she was bored stiff and had nothing better to do.

She'd also been applying moisturizer to her face all morning because it felt as if it had been scrubbed with sandpaper—the aftereffects from the guy she'd made out with on Saturday night. Bob, or Bill—or was it Brett? He was just another good-looking frat boy who wore his baseball cap backward and didn't tuck in his shirt. All those guys looked alike, she thought.

Besides working on her face and hair she'd restlessly passed the time by trying on every piece of clothing she owned. After which she decided to throw out her entire wardrobe and start over.

Mostly, though, she stewed about something she'd gotten in the mail, a photograph of the woman her father was about to marry. Stephanie scowled when she thought of the picture of the young woman: attractive and tall with long blond hair—just her father's type.

The kicker was that the woman was only ten years older than Stephanie. Only ten!

"Can you believe it?" she said acidly, kicking the hallway wall.

She hated the very idea of her. "Kirsten," she repeated the name written on the back of the photo. "Kirsten Keats . . . *Mom?* . . . Oh, please."

Kirsten didn't belong in her family. She was a lowlife, a waitress or something like that.

Stephanie hated her already. She needed to

talk to someone about this young witch who Stephanie felt had stolen her father's affections.

"I love you, Dad," she heard Nancy saying.

Maybe Nancy would understand? Stephanie wondered to herself. My father is about to marry someone new; and hers seems to have met some other lowlife.

She's probably Kirsten's sister, Stephanie thought. So maybe Nancy and I could be friends? We could tack up pictures of our new stepmothers and take turns throwing darts at them.

Nancy put down the phone, and Stephanie took a step toward the lounge, then stopped herself. She was almost going to say something nice, but she swallowed it.

Whoa, what's wrong with me? she asked herself. This marriage thing has gotten me all confused. Me friends with Nancy Drew? Miss America herself? Not in a million years!

Fixing a haughty smile on her lips, Stephanie sashayed into the lounge. "Sounds like you're having man troubles again, honey pie," she purred.

Nancy raised her head. She didn't seem to hear.

Stephanie repeated herself, rolling her eyes. "Forget it," she said.

"What are you talking about?" Nancy asked, confused.

"Men!" Stephanie blurted out. "You and men. First, your boyfriend breaks up with you."

"Ned?" Nancy protested. "Wait a second! He didn't—"

Stephanie cut her off. "Then Peter dumps you and moves clear across campus. And now little ol' daddy. My, aren't we having a string of bad luck."

Nancy looked up from the couch, her mouth open in shock.

Stephanie quickly turned away and examined her nails. "Well, at least someone's going to get some schoolwork done around here. After all, you'll have nothing else to do," she snarled. She waltzed back to her room and slammed the door.

Stephanie stood in front of her mirror, smiling at her reflection. "You're so clever," she whispered.

But somewhere in the back of her brain, something wasn't right. Something was poking at her. The corners of her mouth were lifted in a grin, but her eyes weren't smiling. She thought of Nancy still sitting out in the lounge, thinking of losing her father.

Stephanie licked her lips, trying to clean away the bitter taste in her mouth. She blinked, trying to stop the tears that were threatening to start in her eyes.

"I hate you, Nancy Drew," she whispered. "I hate you, Dad. *All* of you, you're all *losers!*"

When Nancy returned to her room, she was relieved that Kara was finally off the phone. As usual, though, her makeup and cotton balls were strewn all over the books on her desk. She was standing with her head in her closet, a small mountain of clothes growing at her feet.

"Correct me if I'm wrong," Nancy deadpanned, "but didn't you do that yesterday? And the day before?"

Kara shrugged. "I have another study date with Tim, and I keep hoping something spectacular will miraculously appear in my closet. Something I forgot I had."

"I understand completely," Nancy said. As much as Kara annoyed her with her phone hogging and clothes raids, she was always fun.

She's definitely one of a kind, Nancy thought.

All at once Kara was staring at her. "Is there something wrong?"

Kara's always surprising me, Nancy thought. She's smarter than she lets on. . . .

"Oh, nothing." Nancy said. "Stephanie . . ." she started to say.

Kara held up her hands. "Say no more. I ran into the Evil Twin in the bathroom about an hour ago. I don't know what's up with her, but she's definitely on the warpath."

They heard a knock on the suite door.

"Oh no! He's here already!" Kara cried. She started leaping around the room, tiding and arranging things. She yanked open her desk drawer and swept her makeup in on top of her pens and paper; she kicked her clothes into her closet and slammed it shut, grabbed a fistful of underwear, and stuffed it under her pillow. "Quick, Nancy, do me a favor and get the door?"

"Sorry. Expecting someone, are we?" she asked, enjoying Kara's antics.

Frantically struggling with her hair, Kara waved her out. "Nancy! Please?" she begged.

"Okay, okay," Nancy said, smiling. "But you owe me."

"Whatever. Just get the door!"

Nancy raced to the suite door, and said, "Hi, Tim," before she got the door open all the way.

A mortified expression crossed Tim's eyes. "Oh" was all he managed to say.

Nancy led him through the lounge. By the time they reached the room, Kara was standing waiting for them, a smile fixed on her lips. Her hands were clasped in front of her, and she was totally cool, calm, and collected. The linen shift she'd thrown on was attractive. Amazed by Kara's transformation, Nancy smiled in admiration.

Maybe she's a special kind of genius, she considered.

Tim obviously thought so, too. When he saw Kara, his eyes lit up.

"Look what I found at the door," Nancy said.

"Nancy, this is Tim," Kara said. "Tim—"

"We've already met," Tim muttered, reddening.

Kara squinted. "You did?"

Nancy laughed. "Yeah, last night. And we have a world in common."

Tim's expression relaxed, but Kara looked confused.

"Nancy caught me pulling a prank in the library last night," Tim explained to her.

"That was a prank?" Nancy asked.

Tim winced. "I kind of—well, borrowed a globe from the library."

Nancy snorted and rolled her eyes. "Borrowed. That's a good one."

"It was to prove my loyalty to the fraternity house," Tim added quickly. "But don't worry. Chip returned it this morning."

"Chip?" Kara asked. "Who's Chip?"

"I told you I was pledging Alpha Delt," Tim explained. "Chip is the pledge master. He assigns all the pledge pranks—and makes sure they're carried out—with a vengeance."

"He did look kind of scary," Nancy teased.

"How do *you* know all this?" Kara asked her.

"We all met in the library last night. Tim was there with Liz and Daniel."

"You mean you went to the library after our date? And after all the complaining you did last night about how you hate to study!" Kara teased, wagging her finger at Tim.

"I do hate studying. I only went to the library for this prank," Tim promised.

"So what other 'pranks' does O Mighty Pledge

Master have in mind for you?" Nancy asked Tim sardonically.

Tim shifted his feet uncomfortably. "It's all just for fun. Frats have a bad reputation for being harsh on their pledges, but they're never as bad as the stories.

"Don't you have to do anything for Pi Phi?" Tim asked Kara.

Kara shrugged. "Little stuff," Kara answered, "like cleaning the bathroom floor with a toothbrush. It's no big deal."

"You see?" Tim said. "It's all pretty dumb, harmless stuff. You just do it then forget it."

"Unless you're branded a total dork for the rest of your life," Kara said.

"You did look pretty funny sneaking away last night," Nancy pointed out to Tim.

Tim reddened. "It's better than . . ." he started to say, then shut up. He started again. "The Alpha Delts stopped serious hazing almost twenty years ago. They had a bad experience. I'm not totally up on what it was, but I think it had something to do with the Coop."

"You mean that weird-looking brick gazebo thing?" Kara asked.

"It's all boarded up," Nancy added. "It doesn't look as if it's been used in years."

"It hasn't. That's the point," Tim said. "It's been blocked up ever since the hazing incident."

"Did someone get hurt?" Nancy asked.

Tim shook his head. "I don't know. No one

really knows what happened—it was so long ago."

Nancy thought the whole story sounded fascinating. "So nobody goes into the Coop at all now?" she asked.

"No one knows if it's safe anymore," Tim replied. "And the national Alpha Delt charter doesn't want to spend money to fix it up."

"They should just knock it down, then," Kara suggested, "and put in a pool."

Nancy thought Tim was about to say something but stopped himself. "Anyway, that's not why I'm here." He smiled at Kara. "We have a date now. And I also want to invite you to a party at the house tomorrow night. Since you're so interested," Tim continued, turning to Nancy, "why don't you come and see the house for yourself?"

"Thanks," Nancy said. "But I wouldn't want to fall through a trapdoor or anything."

Tim laughed. "Bring along someone else to protect you, as long as she's good-looking!"

Kara slapped Tim playfully.

"Don't worry, Kara," Nancy said, smiling at her roommate, who had managed to make herself incredibly attractive in under thirty seconds. "I don't think you have a thing to worry about."

Tim smiled. "I couldn't agree more."

CHAPTER 5

Nancy was walking across campus toward the Waterman Street Apartments, just off campus behind the freshman dorms. She hadn't slept at all the night before, but for some reason she was wired, surging with energy.

I'm probably just relieved, she thought.

It was Wednesday at 5:03 P.M. Nancy had slipped her English paper under her professor's office door at 4:58. No papers would be accepted after 5:00 sharp. She'd written without a break since the afternoon before. Her brain was mush, her fingers cramped from typing, and she couldn't remember the last time she'd eaten.

My first big college paper, she mused. What a great feeling to have handed it in!

Approaching the apartment house, Nancy finally felt the fatigue tugging at her legs.

"You can't be tired," she commanded herself, thinking of the Alpha Delta mixer in a few hours. After working so hard, she just wanted to party. And since Tim had said she could bring anyone she wanted, she'd decided to bring everyone she knew.

She climbed the steps to the second floor, where Will Blackfeather and Andy Rodriguez lived. As she raised her hand to knock on the door she heard voices—a lot of them.

"They're already *having* a party," Nancy muttered, and walked in. "Hey, everybody!"

George, Will, Andy, and Reva Ross were sitting in a circle on the floor. They were flipping playing cards into the center, as they squinted at their hands and yelled.

Everyone looked up at Nancy and said hello—then went back to their game.

"What're you playing?" Nancy asked George.

George shrugged. "Beats me. I'm just going along with the crowd."

"We're playing Hearts," Andy explained.

Nancy lowered herself next to him and checked out his cards. She liked Andy a lot and thought that he and Reva would make a great couple, if they ever got together. They were both incredibly smart and had similar interests, Nancy knew. Reva and Andy had just put together a guide for Wilder students to learn about the Internet computer network.

Nancy cleared her throat. "Anyone interested

in accompanying a brilliant, ravishing strawberry blond to the Alpha Delt mixer tonight?"

Will and Andy instantly looked up from their game, but Reva frowned. "Ahem," George said loudly. "And who might that be?"

"Why, me, of course!" Nancy laughed.

"Oh," George said dryly.

Nancy pretended to pout. "Don't all say yes at once."

"Sorry, Nancy," Will said, "but George and I are having dinner with her roommate, Pam, and Pam's boyfriend, Jamal."

"And Andy and I just started this computer consulting business," Reva explained. "We're teaching people how to get on-line with the Internet. And we're totally swamped with clients. I don't think we'll be going to any parties for a while."

"And I haven't spent any time with Pam for days," George added.

Nancy nodded. "Bess will be very disappointed."

"Bess?" George asked.

"Apparently Kappa is Alpha Delt's sister house. All the pledges have to act as hostesses at the party. Didn't Bess tell you?"

George shook her head. "I haven't heard from Bess since we had lunch on Monday."

"That's weird," Nancy said, frowning. Bess had just called *her* to make sure she was coming. Why hadn't she called George? That was unlike Bess.

She must still be hurt that George didn't tell her about the camping trip, Nancy surmised.

"I'm sure she tried to call, and the line was just busy," Nancy offered.

"Maybe," George replied. But her expression said, "Yeah, right." Nancy didn't disagree.

" 'Kappas Are Here to Serve,' " Chip read off Bess's T-shirt. "I like the sound of that. What are you offering? Or would you like to tell me in private?"

"Nothing you want," Eileen O'Connor cut in, sticking a cup of soda in Chip's enormous hand. "Here, have this. It'll cool you off."

"Wow, thanks," Chip muttered, peering unenthusiastically into his cup before walking away.

Bess winked at Eileen. Eileen was turning out to be one of the best things about rushing Kappa house. Squarely built, her nose dotted with freckles, Eileen was beautiful in a fresh, farm girl kind of way, Bess thought.

"At first I thought these T-shirts were just stupid," Bess said, "but now I'm starting to think they're dangerous."

Eileen nodded and continued pouring soda.

"Casey Fontaine alert," Eileen whispered.

Bess threw up her hands as she spotted Nancy's redheaded suitemate. "That's all I need, to be embarrassed in front of Casey again!"

Eileen snickered. "I heard about your little recital in front of the entire *Grease!* cast."

Bess rolled her eyes. "Probably the single most mortifying moment of my life. First, Soozie Beckerman demands that I wrangle Casey into joining Kappa, then she purposely disgraces me in front of her. I can't win! I think Soozie's out to ruin my life!"

Eileen nodded in commiseration. "Soozie's out to ruin everyone's life. Every time I see her coming, I run the other way."

Bess watched as Casey twisted through the crowd as a boat cut through water. Bess couldn't help but admire her. Not only was Casey beautiful, with her short, flame-red hair, perfect posture, and a creamy complexion, but she also happened to be very cool about her fame. Hanging out with her was just like hanging out with anyone else.

Well, almost, Bess mused to herself.

"How is she able to ignore the fact that every guy she passes drools all over her?" Bess asked.

"Practice makes perfect," Eileen pointed out.

Casey spotted them behind the drinks table and made a beeline over. "Hey, guys!" she said enthusiastically. "So, the Kappas have you doing their dirty work here, too?" She nodded at Bess and Eileen's shirts.

Bess reddened. "Pretty dumb, huh?"

Casey shrugged. "I don't know. It all seems like fun, actually."

Bess couldn't believe her ears. *"Really? It does?"*

"Well, isn't it?" Casey asked as if she really wanted to know.

"Ow!" Bess cried as Eileen gave her a swift kick under the table.

"I mean, *yeah!*" Bess said, grinning hard. "We're having a ball."

"To tell you the truth," Casey said wistfully, "I sort of miss all the little games and pranks the cast of my show used to pull on one another. Some of them were so funny, the director managed to work a couple of them into the show."

Bess smiled genuinely. If Casey could take pranks in stride, why couldn't she?

Casey was pensive for a second, as if she was deep in thought. "Maybe joining the Kappas *would* be fun," she mused out loud.

"Definitely!" Bess cried, almost beside herself.

Eileen cleared her throat, obviously trying to stay calm. "Absolutely," she said earnestly. "Twenty-four-hour-a-day friends, food, a beautiful house to live in, parties, sisterhood. Joining the Kappas would be the best decision you made at Wilder."

Casey squinted, as if she was trying to picture all those things. "Maybe it would," she said reflectively. "Maybe it would."

Nancy stopped halfway up the hill to the Alpha Delta house, admiring its towering beauty. Perched on top of the hill, with its columns glowing in the evening light, it looked more like a plantation house than a frat house. People were sitting on the railing of the giant, wraparound porch. All of the upstairs windows were alight. Soft music and laughter flowed out of them and down the hillside.

"Looks a little crowded to mix," she murmured.

As she got closer, she noticed a dark, hulking mass in the shadows off to the right. She could make out vines and ivy crawling up the sides and covering the boarded-over windows.

That must be the Coop, Nancy thought. Tim's story had piqued her interest, and she definitely wanted to check it out. But not that night. Right then the music's pull was stronger.

As she made her way through the doorway, Nancy noticed that everyone seemed occupied with someone else; and she suddenly felt weird that she was all alone.

I should have asked someone to come with me, Nancy thought to herself. But who? Bess was already here—somewhere. So was Kara. Maybe she should have asked Jake Collins, her colleague on the *Wilder Times*? Nancy felt funny just thinking it and pushed away the thought before she asked herself why Jake's face had popped so quickly into her mind.

"Hey," Nancy said, spotting Bess at the drinks table and walking over to stand next to her.

Bess was grinning from ear to ear. "Guess

what?" she said excitedly. "Casey's thinking of pledging the Kappas!"

"Wow," Nancy said. "That's unexpected."

"I don't know," Eileen offered, joining them. "I think she's had the idea all along."

"I guess this means you're out of Soozie Beckerman's doghouse," Nancy said to Bess.

Bess shrugged. "At least I have one foot out."

Nancy chose a cup of soda. "Bess, I wanted to ask you about something," she said quietly. "It's about George."

"Maybe later?" Bess said, peeking worriedly over Nancy's shoulder.

"Hi, girls!" Nancy heard someone cry. She turned around to find Soozie Beckerman approaching, with an entourage of freshman pledges following obediently behind her.

"Gotta run," Bess said, disappearing into the crowd.

As Bess escaped, Nancy heard someone call her name.

Nancy saw Kara waving from across the crowded room. She was standing with Tim and Liz and Daniel.

As she made her way over to them Nancy noticed a lot of guys watching her, and she didn't mind. Her fatigue from her first official allnighter had made her punchy—and brave. One guy smiled at her as she went by. He was kind of cute: tall and muscular, and dressed casually in blue jeans and a brown linen shirt—unlike most of the other guys, who were wearing chinos and oxford shirts.

"Ouch!" Nancy said, bumping into the chest of another guy who'd stepped in her path. "Haven't I seen you someplace before?" he asked, leering.

"Good line, very original," Kara said, sweeping over and taking Nancy by the arm. "You seem to have stirred some interest," she wisecracked, tugging Nancy away.

Nancy glanced over her shoulder toward the other guy, the cute one in the blue jeans. He was gazing right at her. Nancy blushed and turned to her friends.

"So, what do you think?" Kara asked meaningfully. "You know, the guys and stuff."

Nancy raised an eyebrow. "Anyone in particular?"

Kara looked exasperated. "Okay, okay, *Tim*. What do you think of him?"

Knitting her brow and tapping her chin with her finger, Nancy barely held in a grin as she spoke.

"Definitely handsome," she said pseudoseriously. "Refreshingly unconcerned about his appearance—that old high school varsity sweatshirt earns him points in the 'book of attitude.' Especially since it's a—gasp!—sweatshirt for the high school varsity band." Nancy nodded. "Two thumbs up," she concluded.

Kara was beaming. "Do you think he likes me?"

"Well, he *has* suffered through two study dates with you, Kara," Nancy joked. "Which I can only assume means you'll both fail your psychology test. And he did invite you tonight."

"And to a dance on Saturday," Kara added, her eyes sparkling.

"And at this very second, he's gazing at you with beautiful, suggestive eyes," Nancy teased.

Kara gasped.

"So," Nancy continued. "I'd say that on the like-you-like-you-not scale of one to ten, he's hovering right around eleven."

"Enough roommate camaraderie," Daniel cut in, wedging himself between Nancy and Kara and herding them back toward the circle.

"So, Nancy, what do you think of Alpha Delt?" Daniel asked as Tim and Liz joined them.

"It's very nice," Nancy replied. "It sure beats dorm living."

"So you think it's worth pledging?" Tim inquired earnestly.

Nancy would have said, Sure, why not? if she hadn't heard the uncertainty in Tim's voice.

Before she could answer, a panel in the wall behind them separated from the rest and swung away, revealing a doorway. Inside, Nancy could see a dimly lit room, with an enormous wooden table and huge chairs upholstered in worn wine-colored fabric. Portraits in gilded frames lined the walls.

Chip Booth filled the doorway with his bulk. He smiled, obviously pleased with the crowd. When a second guy stepped out from behind Chip, Tim and Daniel exchanged looks of wary surprise.

"Having fun?" Chip asked.

"I was expecting everyone to be carrying red gym bags," Nancy joked. No one laughed—except Kara, who was laughing at everything.

Chip wavered, then seemed to recover his sense of humor. "We only carry those when we *steal* something," he said with a laugh. Daniel and Tim joined in the laughter. "But why steal from your own house?" Chip said.

"Good point," the second guy said. He was tall, with thin, dark hair and shining blue eyes that made him appear easily amused. He also had the calm appearance of someone in charge, so when Chip introduced him as John Reed, the Alpha Delta president, Nancy wasn't surprised.

"Who's your friend?" John asked Kara and Liz without taking his eyes off Nancy.

Nancy extended her hand. "Nancy Drew."

"And will the Kappas have the honor of *your* pledge?" he asked hopefully, holding on to Nancy's hand a second longer than necessary.

Nancy stuck her hands safely in her pockets and shook her head. "It's not for me," she said.

"Our loss," John said courteously.

"She may not be interested in sororities," Chip said conspiratorially to John, "but Nancy is very curious about fraternities. Especially our house."

66

"And she should be," John said easily. "She should especially be interested in our president."

"Well," Nancy blushed, not quite sure how to respond to John's obvious flirting. "I wouldn't say I'm uninterested in sororities. One of my best friends, Bess Marvin, is rushing Kappa," Nancy offered. "She's serving drinks—"

"Bess . . . yes," John repeated, still staring at Nancy.

"We'd better split, John," Chip said, leading him away. "We don't have a lot of time."

"Let me know if there's anything Alpha Delt, or its president, can do to make you happy," John said to Nancy.

He grinned charmingly before closing the paneled door and disappearing into the crowd.

As the door was shutting, Nancy caught a glimpse of something in the corner of the secret room. It was the library globe. She threw a glance at Tim, to see if he'd noticed it, too. But he and Daniel were engrossed in quiet conversation.

Huh, Nancy said to herself. Either Tim had lied to her about the globe being returned, or Chip had lied to Tim.

Nancy turned her attention back to her friends. Liz and Kara were involved in a heavy conversation about some obscure point of architectural criticism that Liz had picked up in class—and which Nancy knew Kara wouldn't remember five minutes after Liz finished explaining it.

She turned, smiling, to Tim and Daniel, but

they were leaning against the secret door still talking in whispers.

Nancy shrugged and finished her soda. Her eyes scanned the room for the cute guy in the linen shirt, but she couldn't find him anywhere.

In a lull in the music, she caught snippets of Tim and Daniel's conversation—something "select," and a "secret walk" that Daniel couldn't be a part of because he had to be in the studio all night.

Then one of them cleared his throat, and their conversation stopped instantly.

"So," Nancy said cheerfully, careful not to give away the fact that she'd been eavesdropping. "Anybody want something to drink?"

"Oops!" Kara squealed as she stumbled over a manhole cover outside Thayer Hall. It was late. One by one, lights all over the dorm were going off. "I trip over that thing almost every day. You'd think I'd learn...."

"Actually, I tripped over it yesterday," Tim admitted. "And again tonight, when I came to pick you up."

Then he laughed—a laugh so adorable Kara wanted to kiss him.

They gazed at each other in the moonlight. Kara didn't want to go in, and Tim didn't seem to be in any hurry, either.

"You want to get a cup of coffee somewhere or something?" Kara asked hopefully.

"At one in the morning?" Tim asked dubiously.

Kara smiled foolishly. Tim kicked at the ground. "Actually, I have some stuff I have to take care of at Alpha Delt," he said. "Clean-up duty, you know."

Kara nodded. "Thanks for a great time, Alpha Delt's really cool."

"Thank *you*," Tim insisted. "And Alpha Delt's cooler with you in it."

Kara could swear her heart skipped a beat. She could feel her luck changing before her very eyes. Most of the guys she went out with took her for granted or didn't take her for very much at all. But Tim was sweet and sensitive—even a little insecure. He wasn't afraid to admit his feelings. He seemed to appreciate Kara for what she was, not for what she wasn't. With him, she didn't feel dirty or ignorant or messy. She felt beautiful and smart.

"I guess I'd better get going," he said apologetically. "I have an early class tomorrow."

Kara nodded sadly, though inwardly she was beaming. "Hey, how about breakfast tomorrow morning, after your class?"

Tim's eyes lit up. "You're on! I'll pick you up around ten-fifteen!"

I can't wait, Kara wanted to say. But instead, she waved and whispered, "Thanks again."

Thanks for everything.

CHAPTER 6

Nancy!" someone called, and knocked on her door. "Get up, there's someone at the suite door for you!"

Nancy shook her head. At first, she didn't know where she was. Her clear blue eyes scanned the room, pausing on the clock. Its glowing electronic numbers said 6:30 A.M. The window was filled with dim gray light. A girl was in the bed against the opposite wall, dead asleep. She saw a mountain of discarded clothes in one corner. "Mount Verbeck," Nancy remembered all at once. "Wow, that was one deep sleep."

"Nancy!" the voice called again. It was Dawn Steiger, the suite's resident advisor.

"Coming," Nancy whispered. Then she remembered that Kara could sleep through an army convoy rumbling through their room. "Be right there," she said in full voice.

She pulled on her blue jeans and a T-shirt and opened the door. "What is it? Is anything wrong?"

Dawn was standing unsteadily in her night-gown, eyes closed, her blond hair hanging in front of her face like a curtain. "There's someone at the door," she said groggily.

Nancy remembered her lunch date with her father for that day. "Is it my father?"

"Who? No, it's Jake."

"What could he want so early?"

"I don't know," Dawn muttered. "But it better be important. Good night—"

Nancy walked down the hall and opened the suite door. "What's—"

Jake blustered in before Nancy could finish. "We have to talk," he said breathlessly.

Nancy held back a laugh. Though Jake's brown eyes flashed with concentration, his clothes were rumpled and his brown hair was mussed—he looked like anybody else who'd just gotten out of bed. Only a lot cuter, Nancy noticed.

Nancy had only become friends with him recently. He was a junior and the star reporter for the *Wilder Times,* where Nancy was a cub reporter. He was ultraserious about journalism, but was also kind and funny, and Nancy liked him a lot.

Though not necessarily at six-thirty the morning after a late night at the Alpha Delta party.

"Something just happened, and I have to start

working on a piece for the newspaper right away," he said.

Nancy yawned. "What does that have to do with me?"

Jake frowned. "I need your help."

"It couldn't wait?"

"A good reporter works twenty-four hours a day, even in college," he said.

"Sorry," Nancy said. She knew he was right. News didn't always happen between nine and five. If she really wanted to be an investigative journalist, she had to be ready to go—all the time. "What is it?"

Nancy was tired. If she was going to listen to something, she wanted to be sitting, so she perched herself on the edge of the coffee table.

"Some freshman was just found an hour ago passed out on the grounds of one of the fraternities," Jake said. "He was wearing nothing but a T-shirt and a pair of boxer shorts."

For some reason, Nancy wasn't surprised, with everything she'd heard about fraternities, and the wild frat parties she'd been to herself. "Doesn't that kind of stuff happen all the time?" she asked.

"What doesn't happen all the time is hypothermia. Or alcohol poisoning. He's still unconscious, and he's not waking up."

Nancy gasped. "That's horrible!"

Jake nodded. "I'm starting research. And I was wondering if I could count on you for some help.

All I have so far is the kid's name, Tim Downing—"

Jake's mouth kept moving, but Nancy didn't hear him. All she heard was "Tim Downing— Tim Downing," echoing in her brain. She felt short of breath.

"Nancy?" Jake was saying. "Are you okay?"

Nancy blinked her eyes. "Fine. I'm fine."

Nancy pictured Kara still sleeping soundly, and happily, in her bed. Last night, when she finally came in an hour after Nancy, she was so giddy with happiness she could hardly lie still. Nancy felt terrible. She knew she had to tell Kara.

"So how quickly can you get dressed?" Jake asked.

"I can't go with you, Jake," she said, ushering him toward the door.

"You have someplace to be at six-thirty in the morning?" Jake asked in disbelief.

"I'm really sorry," Nancy said, "but my roommate has been dating Tim Downing. I have to break the news to her."

Jake's jaw dropped open. "Wow. Well, that's a coincidence. Maybe she'll know something."

Nancy shook her head. "I doubt it. When she got in last night, she was so happy."

"Let me know if she does though, okay?" Jake said, moving toward the suite door.

"Okay," she said, getting up. "I'll catch up with you soon." She closed the door behind him.

* * *

Walking across the lobby, Jake felt his stomach give a plaintive rumble. He didn't know if he was hungry, or just nervous. He couldn't deny that he liked Nancy—in fact, he more than liked her. She was a talented journalist, but she was also very beautiful. And smart. And driven. He wouldn't say he was head-over-heels. Then again, he wouldn't say that he'd be that way about anybody.

"But she doesn't seem interested in you," Jake muttered. "For one thing, she probably still has Peter on the brain."

Peter Goodwin had been Jake's freshman roommate, and the two of them were best friends until recently. Jake knew that Nancy and Peter had dated, but weren't together anymore. Now Jake couldn't help but wonder if Nancy was still thinking about Peter.

"Which means that she probably isn't thinking about you," Jake informed himself.

"Patience," he advised himself as he pushed open the front door to the dorm.

It was late morning when Stephanie, Casey, and Eileen sat in the Thayer 301 lounge discussing Tim. Lying across the couch in gym shorts and a halter top, Stephanie sawed at her fingernails with an emery board as she listened to Casey question Eileen.

"So, let me get this straight. No one knows

what happened to Tim?" Casey asked Eileen, who was lying on the floor in her bathrobe.

Eileen shook her head. "Not yet anyway, he's still unconscious."

"How awful. I hope he's going to be all right," Casey said. "I met him at the Alpha Delt party last night. He seemed really sweet. And nuts about Kara."

Stephanie realized she was tired of discussing depressing news. "Let's talk about something else," she said.

"All right, tell me again all the wonderful reasons I should join the Kappas," Casey said to Eileen.

"Well," Eileen said, holding out her hands to count off on her fingers, "there's Bess."

"Uh-huh—"

"There's me."

Stephanie snorted. "How could you resist?"

"There's the sorority house—" Eileen went on.

"A dump," Stephanie muttered.

Casey was laughing. "Stephanie, somewhere below all that meanness and black lipstick and sexy skin is a very sweet little girl."

Stephanie rolled her eyes. "Give me a break."

Just because you're world-famous, and apparently acceptable looking—though I, for one, don't see it—doesn't mean I have to put up with your little niceties, she said to Casey in her mind.

Just the night before Casey had found the photograph of Stephanie's stepmother-to-be and said she looked sweet. Sweet? "I'll show you sweet," Stephanie had replied, enraged, and tore the picture into little bits and threw them in the air like confetti. Casey just stood there unfazed, clucking her tongue. "There goes your plan to hang the picture for target practice," she'd said.

"And then there are the guys," Eileen continued with her list.

"Social Neanderthals," Stephanie mumbled.

"Who are you calling a Neanderthal?" Eileen shot back. "Have you taken a look at your hair this morning?"

Stephanie shot up. "What's wrong with my hair?"

"Nothing—if you like it that way."

"Anyway," Casey said, stepping in like a referee, "Neanderthal or not—I already have a guy."

Stephanie racked her brain for something witty to say, but found zilch. The fact was, Casey had a totally hot boyfriend, Charley Stern, her costar from *The President's Daughter*. Half the female population in America would probably drop dead in his presence.

There was a knock on the door. No one moved. "Anyone expecting someone?" Eileen said.

"It's probably the Kappa Queen herself, coming to make you cartwheel across campus in your nightgown." Stephanie laughed.

"Whoever it is better not mind the sight of

females in repose," Casey said, stretching herself across the floor.

"Sounds good!" the voice on the other side of the door said.

Casey leaped to her feet.

"Who is it?" Eileen asked, alarmed.

Stephanie got to the door first, and as soon as she got it half open, her jaw dropped.

"Charley!" Casey shrieked, pushing by Stephanie and launching herself into Charley Stern's arms.

Eileen was grinning from ear to ear. But Stephanie was mortified. Here was probably the best-looking guy in the whole country and she was dressed in total trash, without makeup, without gel or hair wax or spray or *anything* in her hair! She wanted to scream. Or run away.

But she couldn't move. He was too gorgeous to believe.

"You look even better in person than you do in the magazines," Eileen said, smiling and holding out her hand. "I'm Eileen O'Connor, one of Casey's suitemates."

Stephanie would have agreed with Eileen—if she'd ever agreed with Eileen about anything before. Which she hadn't. And which she had no plans to do in the near future. But Charley *was* incredible. He was muscled in an attractive, subtle way and had thick glossy hair and piercing eyes.

"Charley Stern," Charley said, shaking Eileen's hand. He turned to Stephanie. "And you are?"

Stephanie was struck dumb because he was seeing her in all her morning decrepitude.

"What, you speechless?" Eileen teased her.

"This is my roommate, Stephanie Keats," Casey said, putting an arm around Stephanie. "She's got a little vocal problem right now. Don't mind her. At times like this, we communicate through hand signals."

Casey made fluttering movements with her hands in front of Stephanie's face, to the howling delight of Eileen.

"Okay, okay," Stephanie said. "I can talk. Hi," she said to Charley, barely looking him in the eye.

"So, how's my favorite TV girlfriend?" Charley said, stepping past Stephanie and taking Casey in his arms. He planted a long, decidedly non-TV kiss on her lips.

Stephanie hid her eyes. Great, she thought. Not only do I have to live with Miss Famous and Popular, but now her gorgeous hunk of a boyfriend is here.

"What's all the noise about?" Reva said, popping her head out of her room.

"It's Charley!" Eileen announced.

Reva appeared in her bathrobe, a towel twisted swamilike atop her head. "I like your work," she said confidently, shaking Charley's hand, as Casey introduced them.

"Thanks," Charley said, blushing.

"Tell Reva about your new computer," Casey prodded him. "She's our local computer whiz."

"You like computers?" Reva asked.

"I just got hooked up to the Internet," Charley explained. "I get some of my fan mail through e-mail now. Responding to e-mail is a lot easier than writing thirty letters a day.

"I spend a lot of time each week just answering questions about what shampoo I use and what my dream date would be like."

Casey hooked him around the waist. "It better be a *lot* like me," she said, grinning.

"How do you know it's not just one girl sending you a lot of letters under different names?" Stephanie asked.

"Who'd do that?" Charley asked.

Suddenly Stephanie was hit with a brilliant idea. If she learned how to use a computer, she could talk to her roommate's gorgeous boyfriend through e-mail while Famous Miss Perfect Fontaine sat right across the room.

I wonder if they're really as happily-ever-after as they seem to be? Stephanie schemed. They *are* actors, after all. How do I know they're not faking it? Maybe the famous and talented Charley Stern would rather be going out with someone else. Someone with more depth and character than Casey. Someone like me.

There's only one way to find out, she decided. What another genius idea!

*　　*　　*

"What's going on out there?" Bess asked Ginny, eyeing Ginny's closed door.

Ginny shrugged. "Random cries and high-pitched laughter. Not unusual for Suite Three-oh-one."

Bess and Ginny were sitting in Ginny's room, Ginny at her neatly arranged desk, her biology notes in an orderly pile next to her elbow. Bess was sprawled on Liz's bed, her notes and pens and candy-bar wrappers and other unidentifiable junk cascading out of her book bag and surrounding her in a jumble.

Blowing a wisp of golden hair out of her eyes, Bess leaned back against Liz's pillows. "I still can't believe it about Tim."

Ginny shook her head sadly. "You should have seen Kara. She and Nancy ran out of here to the university clinic at seven this morning."

"It's so sad," Bess lamented. "They still don't know anything?"

Ginny squinted out the window. "I wonder if Liz knows—"

A sudden thought came to Bess. When she first got there half an hour ago, there was no sign of Liz. Her bed was neatly made, and her desk looked as if it hadn't been touched in days.

"Speaking of running out of here," Bess commented, "where *is* Liz?"

Ginny sighed. "A secret potion has transformed her from a funny but strange human being to a series of yellow Post-it notes, usually scribbled at three in the morning—or whenever it is she comes back to sleep."

Bess grinned. "Could that secret potion possibly be male in character?"

"I think it's called architecture madness," Ginny replied. "Anyway," she said sternly, "it's time for some mambo studying. You did well on that makeup test last week." She eyed the mess surrounding Bess. "But I'm declaring you an official disaster zone and making you a personal project. You're going to get a *B* in biology if I have to keep you up studying all night."

Bess laughed, her eyes shining. "Yes, sir—I mean, *ma'am*," she said happily—relieved that someone was taking an interest in her work. With Ginny keeping watch over her shoulder, she didn't feel so alone.

When Bess arrived at college, she knew she was prepared for the frat parties and the mixers—all the really great stuff she'd heard about and looked forward to since high school. But books? Class schedules?

After a couple of C's and almost D's, she knew that if she didn't do something about her study habits she might not be around to enjoy all the stuff she *really* came to college for.

"I'm glad you're my tutor, Gin," Bess said affectionately.

Ginny smiled, and was about to say something else, when more laughter seeped under the door.

Ginny threw down her book. "That does it. I'm going out there."

"Me, too," Bess said, leaping up, happy to take a break—even if they hadn't started yet.

She was pining for excitement, and by the time she and Ginny reached the lounge, she'd constructed a scene in her mind in which Stephanie and Casey were yanking each other's hair out.

But when she turned the corner and faced who was really there, the blood drained from her face.

"Charley Stern!" she whispered hoarsely.

Ginny was grinning from ear to ear. "Hi!"

Casey introduced the two girls to the handsome star. She draped her arm around Bess. "Bess is in the chorus of *Grease!* with me," she told Charley proudly. "Wilder has some real talent here," she said, squeezing Bess's shoulder.

Bess could feel her face heat up. She thought she might faint.

"Laying it on a bit thick?" Stephanie said.

Casey shrugged. "Not at all. Bess is good."

"Okay, Case," Bess murmured, growing more embarrassed by the second.

"Not only that," Casey said, grinning and rumpling Bess's hair, "but Bess is trying to get me a late invitation to the best sorority on campus."

Bess was stunned. "I am? I mean, I *am!*" I can't believe Casey really wants to join the Kappas, she thought.

Bess saw Ginny standing unnoticed against the

wall. "Did you guys hear that Ray's band may be getting a record deal?" Bess blurted out.

Ginny smiled gratefully. Bess knew Ginny would have wanted everyone to know, but was too modest to say it herself.

Charley suddenly looked interested. "I'm really into music. What's the band's name?"

"The Beat Poets," Ginny said.

"Cool name!" Charley exclaimed. "What do they play?"

"It's kind of hard to describe," Ginny said.

Casey gripped Charley's arm. "They're *very* original, Charley," she said. "And Ginny's boyfriend is going to be big."

Charley nodded, impressed. "You guys should know that Casey has a special knack for picking out talent. If she says someone is really good, that someone *is* really good."

Ginny looked totally floored by the compliments. "Thanks. But maybe you should hear them before deciding."

Charley was nodding. "Great idea. I can't wait."

Bess was leaning against the wall, her arms folded, happily gazing at Charley.

This beat studying any day.

CHAPTER 7

The Wilder University clinic sprawled across a couple of blocks at the edge of the campus. By the time Nancy returned with something to drink for Kara, the waiting room downstairs was a lot more crowded. She recognized some of the people milling around as brothers and pledges from Alpha Delta. They all looked unhappy.

Nancy kept picturing Tim lying in the bed upstairs, unconscious and alone. She didn't know him that well, but she did have a great time with him and Kara, and Liz and Daniel last night. And the thought that something happened to him right after she saw him was creepy and sad.

Seeing Kara so upset was really awful. Kara was already crazy about Tim, even after such a short time. As annoying and quirky as her roommate sometimes was, she was also a lovable and dependable friend. Nancy's heart went out to her.

Nancy saw Kara, Liz, and Daniel huddled with Chip and John Reed in a corner of the waiting room. "Hi," she said, putting an arm around Kara. "Any news yet?"

Daniel sat wearily on the arm of an empty chair, raking a hand through his dark hair. "Tim hasn't woken up, and the doctor said that his body temperature is still below normal."

"Tim's such a good guy," Kara said tearfully.

"Yeah," Chip said, looking around the room at the collection of frat brothers. "We all sort of feel responsible, him being a pledge and all."

"And no one knows anything definite?" Nancy asked.

"The nurse just told us that Tim has alcohol poisoning," Daniel said. "Supposedly, he drank an entire bottle of something."

Nancy pictured Tim the night before, standing in their little circle of friends, throwing back his head in cheerful laughter. Almost everyone else in the room was drinking beer and wine, but she distinctly remembered Tim drinking cola.

"But Tim said he never drank," Kara said insistently. "And I can vouch that he had nothing but soda all night last night."

"Well, obviously you're wrong," John Reed said. "Or maybe he drank after the party."

"It doesn't sound like him," Kara said. "When we walked back to Thayer last night, he seemed so happy."

"And what's really weird," Daniel added, "is

that his clothes were soaking wet when he was found."

"He went for a swim?" Nancy asked. "It sounds unbelievable."

Kara nodded in agreement. "You're telling me."

While they were talking, Nancy saw a nurse pull John Reed aside. The woman put something in his hand and whispered in his ear. But Nancy made out what she said: "He was wearing it when he was found."

"Can I take a look at that?" Nancy asked.

John handed it to her, and Nancy turned it over in her palm. It was a neck chain with a small silver medallion, with an *S* carved into the center in Gothic script. It was heavy and looked old, very old.

"Anybody know what the *S* might stand for?" Nancy asked the group.

They all shook their heads.

Nancy looked at Daniel, but he seemed distracted. Nancy knew how close he and Tim were. She didn't want to intrude on his privacy, but since Daniel was the closest to him personally, maybe he'd know something.

"Any ideas?" she asked him gently.

Daniel just shook his head.

"Are you okay?" she asked.

Daniel smiled tightly. "Been better."

Nancy nodded. She wanted to ask him what he'd seen the night before, if anything. But then

Chip and John came over, and Nancy knew Daniel wouldn't say much in front of them.

She walked over to Kara and put an arm around her shoulder. "Do you know where Tim's dorm room is?" she asked.

Kara blinked tearfully. "Yeah, we went there the other night and goofed around with his roommate, Frank. Why?"

Nancy shrugged. "Just a hunch. Say I have an idea. Maybe we should go over to Tim's room and get some of his clothes and things. He'll need them when he regains consciousness," Nancy suggested, trying to give Kara a reason to feel positive.

"Good," Nancy said as Kara nodded. "What do you say we go over there now?"

Kara led Nancy across campus to Tim's dorm, but didn't say much. Nancy didn't ask any questions, but her mind was racing.

She had a bad feeling about this—none of the facts seemed to make it an accident. Tim wasn't a drinker, but his blood alcohol level was off the charts. And why would he have gone swimming at two in the morning, *after* dropping off Kara? Then he was found outside Alpha Delta . . .

Kara brought Nancy to one of the older dorms on campus, Jasper Hall. The rooms were smaller, the painted walls a little dirtier. It wasn't as nice as Thayer Hall, and it lacked the charm of George and Bess's dorm, Jamison.

Tim's room was on the second floor. Kara knocked, and the door opened.

"Hi, Frank," Kara said. "This is Nancy."

Frank was short, unathletic looking, and unsuccessfully trying to grow a goatee.

"Sorry about Tim," Nancy said.

"I thought we could get some clothes and things for Tim and take them back to the hospital," Kara said.

"Sure," Frank replied. "But I was heading over to the registrar to help track down his parents," he added. "Supposedly, they've been on vacation, so they've asked me to help find a relative or neighbor who might have a phone number so the school can reach them. Do you mind getting the stuff together yourselves?"

"No, do you mind?" Nancy asked.

Frank shook his head no and pointed to an old bureau on one side of the room.

"That's his dresser there. I think his shaving stuff and toothbrush are on top, and his clothes are in the closet on the right." Frank took off, leaving them alone.

"It's weird being here with Tim in the hospital," Kara said.

Nancy looked around at what seemed to be a typical freshman room—a few posters of sports stars were on the walls, and textbooks and notes were scattered over his desk.

On the far corner of his desk, Nancy noticed

a beautiful wooden box. It was too big for cigars but too small for much else.

Kara was taking clothes from the closet and putting a small pile together on the bed.

Nancy didn't want to poke around too much, but she did pick up the box and crack the lid to peek inside. There was a torn piece of notebook paper. Nancy glanced at Kara and quickly took a look. There was a single sentence hand-lettered in the same Gothic style as the medallion. "You have been selected," it read.

Nancy closed the box and sat down beside the clothes pile on the bed, staring at the box.

Selected? she pondered. Selected for what?

If she didn't know any better, she would have thought it sounded like a threat.

A threat she contemplated. Did somebody carry it out last night?

"How about some lunch?" Andy asked, reaching for a stack of pizzeria menus.

"How about some breakfast first?" Reva replied, arching her back and yawning.

Andy pinched the bridge of his nose. "You mean we didn't eat anything yet today? It's almost noon!"

They were sitting in Andy's bedroom in his and Will's apartment in the Waterman Street Apartments in front of Andy's new computer set-up. They stacked all their software manuals and copies of the Internet Guide they had put together on a table by the door. It looked like a real consultant's office!

"Are you guys alive in there?" George called from the living room, where she and Will were pretending to do homework.

Andy opened the door a crack, cried, "Barely!" closed it again, and collapsed on his bed.

"Did you ever think that our one little ad in the *Wilder Times* about computer consulting would create this much business?" Reva asked, amazed.

Andy held up that day's schedule of clients and groaned. "Four down—four more to go."

Though she was tired of talking about hard drives and modems, Reva felt like jumping for joy. "Andy, you're going to be able to afford that new computer in just a few weeks!"

Andy smiled wearily. "But will I be alive to use it?" he quipped. "My fingers are starting to seize up."

Reva stepped over, sat Andy up, kneeled behind him, and started kneading his shoulders. "Poor baby," she said jokingly. "Don't complain so much. You'll jinx us. Business is booming!"

"Ooh, there, no *there*," Andy groaned, directing Reva's hands to different spots on his upper back.

Reva was grinning. She and Andy were getting to be better friends, that was for sure. But it was obvious to her that they were getting closer in other ways, too.

While they were putting together the Internet Guide, she'd started to feel little jolts of electricity fly between them. Reva doubled Andy over and massaged his lower back.

She liked being in the same room with him. She liked hearing him talk about computers. He was such a good teacher, patient and funny.

"And beautiful," she whispered.

"What?" Andy asked, lifting his head.

Reva reddened. "I said it's such a beautiful day," she said quickly.

Andy was laughing.

"What's so funny?" Reva asked defensively, thinking he was laughing at her.

"I was just thinking that we'll have to cut back on clients or move in together. Ow!"

"What!"

"Your finger just speared me!"

Reva smiled. Without realizing it, she'd been digging into Andy's back muscles harder and harder. "Maybe that's not such a bad idea," she said thoughtfully.

"What, killing me?" Andy asked.

"Uh, oh," Reva said, trying to sound casual. "I was talking about moving in."

Reva could feel Andy's shoulders stiffen in her hands. He turned his head and looked her in the eyes. Reva thought she was going to melt.

"For business," she said, and laughed.

I knew I liked him, she thought to herself. But maybe it's more than that . . .

Neither of them said a thing. Reva's eyes traveled down his face, pausing on his lips. The silence was growing. Reva felt herself leaning toward him. Andy's fingers touched the tips of hers—

The doorbell rang.

"I thought we were done for the morning," Reva said.

Andy glanced at their schedule. "We are," he said.

"Andy!" Will called. "It's for you. She says she has an emergency!"

"It better be," Andy growled, reluctantly drawing away from Reva and leaving the room.

As Reva settled back into her chair, her heart was pounding. She didn't ever remember feeling this way about a guy.

"We have a new client," Andy said in a funny tone of voice.

"What can we do for you?" Reva asked, and started to turn around.

"A lot," the new client said.

Reva lifted her head, startled by the sight of that all-too-familiar voice, that sleek body, that piercing, sarcastic gaze. "Stephanie?"

As soon as Will settled into the couch again, with his notes, George leaned back into his arms.

"It's so weird that Stephanie has this sudden urge to learn about computers," she said quietly.

"Weird, suspicious, and dubious," Will replied.

"Maybe she wants to learn how to organize all those nasty thoughts floating around her brain," George said.

"Shh, I have to study now," Will said, kissing George on the ear. "So do you."

George pried apart Will's arms. "What I *have* to do is get a tall glass of orange juice—with ice."

"Get me one, too?" Will said, grinning slyly.

George narrowed her eyes with mock irritation. "I *thought* so. Sneaky boy."

George went into the kitchen humming to herself. She couldn't have been happier. She knew that what she and Will had done together was wonderful, but she was a little worried about how they'd act afterward.

But Will and she were as joky and fun together as always—if not more so.

While pouring the orange juice, George heard Stephanie's grating voice float in from the other room. She was going on and on about e-mail, asking Andy and Reva to explain everything twice. "Are you totally, absolutely sure it's private?" Stephanie wanted to know, for the fourth time.

Suddenly the bedroom door swung open, and Andy blew out of the room, flying past George, to the refrigerator. "I wonder if the vegetable crisper would hold me for a few hours?" he muttered.

George laughed. "She's tough, huh?"

Andy growled and beat his forehead with the palm of his hand. "What *planet* is she from?"

Suddenly Stephanie filled the kitchen doorway with her slinky body. Bracing herself against the door frame, Stephanie lifted her arms to reveal a skimpy halter top under her coat. She had a cigarette in her mouth.

"There's no smoking—" George started to say.

"What? Okay, whatever," Stephanie said, flicking her cigarette into the sink. "Hey, Andy, tell me again how this e-mail thing works?" she asked in her sultry voice.

Stubbing out Stephanie's still lit cigarette in the sink, Andy smiled in spite of himself. "Well," he said patiently, "it's just like typing a letter, except instead of mailing it, you send it through the telephone wires."

Stephanie was gazing at him with tremendous interest, obviously not hearing a word.

Uh-oh, George thought. I know that look. The girl is on the prowl.

George glanced into Andy's room. Reva was sitting in front of the computer.

Stephanie left her perch at the door and, totally ignoring George, leaned against the counter right beside Andy. Her arm brushed against his. "You're *such* a wonderful teacher," she purred, picking at his shirt. "What else do you teach?"

94

George couldn't believe it. Both she and Reva were no more than ten feet away! Stephanie would stop at nothing.

"Hey, where's my juice?" Will said as he squeezed into the crowded kitchen. "What's going on in here, a party?"

George wasn't smiling. She and Will glared at Stephanie, who was practically all over Andy.

His face flushed crimson, Andy walked by, mouthing "Help!" at Will and George, before fleeing into his room. Stephanie followed in hot pursuit.

Will could barely contain his laughter. "It looks like she was here for more than e-mail lessons."

"Really!" George said with feigned surprise. "Why would you say that?"

The door to Andy's room slammed shut, and they could hear Stephanie's high-pitched voice barking orders again.

Will pursed his lips. "I don't know. It just fell out of my mouth."

George leaned her face against Will's arm. His skin was warm and soft. "She doesn't know what it means to have someone really care for her."

"I hope *you* know," Will said, hugging George tighter.

CHAPTER 8

After dropping off Kara back at the hospital, Nancy went on to Alpha Delta. She was hoping to find Daniel there and talk to him alone about the strange circumstances of Tim's accident.

But as soon as Nancy reached Alpha Delta, she couldn't help being drawn to the odd little building everyone called the Coop.

The sun shone brightly, casting moving shadows of leaves and vines all over its sides. Nancy walked around it, looking for the entrance. It took a while to find, because it was almost completely covered over with what looked like twenty years of tangling ivy.

Nancy pulled on the old wrought-iron handle, but the door didn't even squeak. There was cement plastered all around the edges of the door.

The door handle was rusty, and Nancy wiped the rusty orange dust onto her jeans.

Obviously, the door had been shut for a very long time. Nancy thought again of what Tim had said about the hazing accident that had taken place inside.

If the Alpha Delta brothers had once used the Coop as a secret meeting place, what did they use now, Nancy wondered. Then she remembered the secret room behind the paneled wall—the room with the huge table and chairs. No doubt that was where any official, secret fraternity meetings took place.

I bet this little building was beautiful when it was in use. Nancy was noticing all the intricate details partially hidden under the vines, including the beautiful little stained glass windows high up on the walls.

Nancy heard a frantic chittering noise and saw a squirrel with a nut in its mouth hanging from a tree branch and scratching at one of the broken windows. It was trying to push its way through the patch on the old window.

The squirrel continued scratching in vain at the piece of cardboard covering the hole. The cardboard was held in place by heavy-duty black duct tape.

"That's weird," Nancy said when she realized that the cardboard had been taped to the window—from the inside.

Just then Nancy felt a hand on her shoulder

and whirled around, startled. When she saw it was Daniel, she began to laugh.

"Sorry," Nancy choked out. "You caught me by surprise."

Daniel smiled, but for once, Nancy didn't sense his usual warmth. "What are you doing here?" he asked casually. Nancy thought she saw his gaze flick nervously to the broken window she'd just spotted.

"Actually," Nancy admitted, "I came here to see you."

"You did?" Daniel replied a little too quickly.

"Yeah, I came to ask you a few things. About Tim." Nancy saw Daniel's smile fade instantly and a shadow cross his eyes.

"It's terrible what happened to him," Daniel said softly, running a hand through his black hair. He took his glasses off for a moment and rubbed the bridge of his nose. "I stared at drawings all last night and today since I left the hospital," he offered, "and my eyes feel like they're about to fall out."

"You don't have any idea what might have happened to Tim after the party do you?" Nancy continued, ignoring his change of subject. "I thought I heard you mention something about plans last night, so I just wondered."

"Plans?" Daniel seemed startled. "No, like I said, I was in the architecture studio all night after the party. Big project due."

Nancy nodded. "Okay," she said calmly, "just

one other thing. Have you ever heard the phrase 'You have been selected'?"

"Where did you hear that?" Daniel asked, surprised. "I mean, that sounds pretty weird," he said, trying to cover quickly.

Nancy shrugged. She was sure that Daniel knew something that he wasn't telling. At least, not yet.

"Well," she said, "if you do find out anything more about the accident, please let me know. I know Kara's pretty worried about Tim."

"I'm sure he'll be fine," Daniel said, steering Nancy away from the Coop and away from the Alpha Delta house.

"Tell me what you know, she wanted to say, but she could see that Daniel was nervous. And worried.

He waved goodbye and went back toward the house. Watching him, Nancy realized that he'd managed to steer her right down the driveway to the street. Was Daniel hiding something? Nancy wondered.

Nancy had lots of questions, but now wasn't the time to get the answers. She checked her watch and headed for campus. She had only twenty minutes before she was supposed to meet her father at Les Peches for lunch.

Nancy felt a little knot in her stomach. She knew how important this meeting would be and how much Carson wanted Nancy and his girlfriend, Avery, to get along.

I'm sure we'll like each other, Nancy told herself firmly as she hurried down the Walk toward town. But then another thought came to her. What if we don't?

"Now, you're *sure* you understand how important this meeting is?" Soozie Beckerman asked for the eleventh time. "You're in charge of telling all the other pledges, so don't let them, or us, down," she warned.

"I know, I know," Eileen said calmly and with a smile. "All pledges *must* attend," she repeated. "Tomorrow night. We'll be there. I promise."

"Good," Soozie said. "You'd better be, or the whole pledge class will be dropped."

"Yes, ma'am," Eileen teased, looking over at the other Kappa sister in the room and grinning conspiratorially. Holly Thornton was a junior, as well as a member of the Kappa Cabinet. She'd been part of the pledge committee, which chose Eileen, Bess, and the other new pledges.

"So?" Soozie asked, staring at Eileen as if she were some alien life-form. "What are you still doing here? You've got eleven pledges to talk to. You'd better get moving!"

Eileen scrambled out of her chair and practically ran for the front door of the Kappa house. Soozie really was amazing, Eileen thought. It was like someone had poured her out of a mold that said Nasty But Popular Sorority Girl. At least Soozie was the only bad thing about the Kappa sorority. Most of the girls were more like Holly. In other words, they were normal and fun. And even if Soozie was pretty mean, she *had* chosen Eileen to be the unofficial leader of the pledge class. I must have something going for me, Eileen mused happily, to make the Great Sooz single me out.

Eileen ran up the front steps of Jamison Hall and headed for the second floor, where Bess lived. Bess was the pledge Eileen got along with best, and she was dying to gossip with her about this incredibly mysterious meeting scheduled for the next night.

"Okay, Kappa pledge!" Eileen called out as she knocked on Bess's door. "I have some top secret confidential Kappa information!"

The door opened just a crack, and Eileen saw a thin slice of Bess's grimacing face.

"Shhh," Bess whispered, finally sticking the top half of her body out into the hallway. "My roommate is studying, and she's been complaining all day about how noisy I am."

"You? Noisy?" Eileen teased. "Not a chance. Anyway, can I come in?"

"Just for a minute," Bess muttered. "And believe me, a minute will be more than you'll want to bear."

"I just came over to tell you about a big Kappa pledge meeting tomorrow night," Eileen said excitedly, following Bess into the room. "We all have to be there, and apparently it's very hush-hush."

"Then I'm sure Bess won't be very welcome," a voice remarked from the other side of the room. Eileen glanced over and saw a preppy-looking girl seated at a desk with a huge text-book, a carefully aligned legal pad, a ruler, a pen-cil, and a highlighter pen. Her long brown hair was pulled severely off her face in a high ponytail.

"Eileen, this is Leslie King," Bess murmured, refusing to look in her roommate's direction.

"She couldn't tell you the meaning of *hush-hush* if you opened the dictionary for her," Leslie continued icily.

"Well, I know it's hard to study with noise," Eileen said, suppressing a smile. "And I can un-derstand your frustration."

"Finally, someone who appreciates the envi-ronment needed for serious study!" Leslie cried, almost sounding gossipy. She fixed on Eileen and began listing Bess's infractions. "First she had a giggly whispered conversation with that theater pal of hers. Then an interminable ten minutes of toenail clipping, followed by half an hour of paper shuffling. And there was the crackly bag of corn chips—"

"You are kidding, aren't you?" Eileen asked. "I mean, a girl's gotta live!"

"I would have to disagree," Leslie replied.

"But Bess told me you're premed!" Eileen

said. "Excuse me if it's not my place, but you might try working on your bedside manner if you don't want all your patients to wind up in the mental ward, playing checkers."

While Leslie's jaw dropped, Eileen took advantage of the silence to grab Bess by the arm and pull her toward the door. "Come on, babe," Eileen said in a gruff voice. "I'm breaking you outta here. Grab your coat!"

Bess grinned and let herself be pulled through the door into the hallway.

"Thanks, I needed that." Bess laughed, giving Eileen a hug. "Now tell me more about this secret meeting!"

"You bet," Eileen said, as they hooked arms and started down the hall. No wonder you want to rush, Eileen thought to herself. If *I* lived with that, I'd want to find a new home, too!

When Nancy got to Les Peches she saw her father's salt-and-pepper hair through the window. Carson Drew had his back to the window, and he was leaning over a table to speak to an attractive woman with soft waves of shoulder-length brown hair. That must be Avery, Nancy thought, trying the woman's name out in her mind.

Nancy took advantage of the opportunity to watch them for a moment. She didn't really want to spy, but she knew that in just a few minutes they'd all be so nervous and careful that they might not act naturally. And Nancy wanted to see how Carson and Avery got along when she wasn't around.

Avery was saying something to Carson, and through the glass, Nancy could hear the familiar sound of her father's deep laughter. She watched as Carson reached out and covered one of Avery's hands with his own. Instinctively, it seemed, Avery turned her palm up and their fingers entwined. Nancy stepped back from the window.

She felt a little ashamed, as if she'd intruded on a very intimate moment. It was obvious that Avery cared for Carson Drew very much. Nancy felt the knowledge sit strangely in her. She couldn't help the prickles of jealousy she felt, but it also made her happy to know her father might be loved by someone special.

"Well, you can't put it off forever, Nancy Drew," she told herself as she pulled open the door and stepped inside the quiet, tastefully decorated bistro.

Nancy had no trouble smiling as she approached Carson's table, because seeing her father always made her incredibly happy.

"Nancy!" Carson cried, standing up and wrapping her into a deep, comfortable hug. "I've missed you so much, I feel like the house is practically empty!"

"The house is never empty with Hannah around," Nancy replied good-naturedly, referring to the Drews' longtime housekeeper, Hannah

Gruen. "And besides, it's not as though I haven't been away from home before."

"That's true," Carson said, holding Nancy at arm's length. "But this time, you're away at college. And that means much more than just being away on a trip or a vacation, or tracking down some dangerous criminal." He chuckled. "Nancy, I'd like you to meet someone very special," Carson continued, turning to his table companion. "This is Avery Fallon."

Nancy couldn't miss the warmth in her father's voice, and when she held out her own hand to Avery, she almost understood right away why Carson was so smitten. Not only was Avery an incredibly beautiful woman, she also radiated a sense of clearheadedness and peace.

"Nice to meet you, Nancy," Avery said, her grip cool and firm. "Of course, I've heard so much about you. But it's nice to put all of the incredible stories together with a real face. Now that I see you, it's not hard to believe they're all true."

Nancy couldn't help but smile at the compliment, though she definitely didn't feel as if Avery was fishing for her admiration in any way.

"Thanks." Nancy smiled as they sat back down. "But I wouldn't believe it all so easily," Nancy teased. "Carson Drew has been known to exaggerate on a few occasions."

"Not about you two," Carson said.

"Well, I hope not." Avery teased back. "But

this time Nancy and I will have to feel each other out without you, Carson." Avery looked back at Nancy with clear honest eyes. "My feeling is already pretty good, though. So, let's order some lunch. I'm starved!"

Nancy had to laugh. Avery's certainly not trying to win me over, Nancy realized. And she's not shy about dealing with anything difficult or uncomfortable.

Avery and Carson started looking over the menu, and Nancy listened as they discussed the options with the comfortable air of a married couple. Avery cracked a joke that made Carson laugh, and after only a few minutes, Nancy had to admit that her father seemed happier than ever.

No, she realized suddenly, it was more that he was happy in a new way—a kind of happy Nancy had never seen before. It was a new Carson Drew who sat beside her. Her father was a man in love.

"Well, certainly, Mr. Blackfeather, you can buy me a diamond anytime," George drawled, fluttering her eyelashes in a very bad southern belle imitation.

"When you look at me like that, I feel ready to do it now," Will replied, leaning down to place a soft kiss on her curving lips.

"Why is it that window shopping with you is *so* much better than the real thing with anyone else?" George grinned. She glanced once more into the jewelry store window display. It may be romantic to tease about, she thought, but I'm not ready for a ring. One step at a time is enough.

"The reason everything is so much better with me," Will explained as he linked George's arm through his, "is because I'm just an exceptional human being. Incredibly handsome, highly intelligent, and tremendously amusing and entertaining."

"Modest to a fault with a teeny, tiny ego," George added somberly.

"And it's better than listening to Stephanie torment Andy and Reva," Will finished.

"Uh-oh," George said, stopping in her tracks.

"Uh-oh is right," Will replied. "What's wrong with my being in love with you?"

George just shook her head.

"George?" Will asked anxiously. "What is it?"

Then he turned around and saw what had made George stop.

"Isn't that Nancy?" Will asked, pointing at the small group gathered in front of Les Peches.

"And her father," George nodded.

"The famous Carson Drew you are always talking about?" Will grinned. "Great! I can't wait to meet him."

Will started to walk, but he stopped as soon as he realized George wasn't with him. He turned back to her with a questioning look.

"George?" He stepped closer to her. "Don't you want to introduce me?"

"Sure." George nodded, not moving forward.

"Yeah." Will looked hurt. "It really seems like it. I mean, hold back your excitement a little."

"Oh, Will." George grabbed his arm. "It's not that I'm embarrassed of *you* or anything. I've told him about you already. It's just that I'm a little—embarrassed—about us." George looked at him meaningfully. "I've known Carson my whole life. It's going to be like introducing you to my father, and we just—we just—"

"We're just in love?" Will added, grinning. "Isn't that what you were going to say?"

George stared into his deep brown eyes. Exactly, she thought. That's exactly it.

"George? Will?" A voice suddenly called out to them. "Hey, you two, over here!"

George saw Nancy waving them over. It's now or never, George thought.

"You're not having any regrets about us, are you?" Will suddenly asked, putting his hands on her arms and staring deeply into her eyes.

George took a moment. Was she? Was that why she was so nervous about introducing Carson to Will?

She smiled, as she realized the truth. "Nope. No regrets." George took Will's hand and they walked over to Nancy, Carson, and Avery.

"Hello, George," Carson said, his blue eyes twinkling as he took in the very tall and muscular young man by her side. George felt a blush start on her cheeks.

"This must be Will." Carson put a hand out. Will took it immediately.

"Very nice to meet you, Mr. Drew," Will said politely.

"Carson, please," he replied quickly. "We're all family here. And this is Avery Fallon," Carson said, introducing her to Will.

"Very nice to meet you," Will replied.

It wasn't as bad as I thought, George realized, as the conversation continued. And now she understood why. She was still the same person on the outside. The only differences were for her and Will to know about, George thought with a grin.

CHAPTER 9

Liz was staring blankly at the wall of her cubicle in Rand Hall. It was Friday morning, and everyone around her was working diligently. Tacked up in front of her were some preliminary sketches for her own project, but she hadn't looked at them for what felt like hours.

All she could think about was Tim. He still hadn't regained consciousness, and the doctors said he might stay that way for days—if not longer!

What bothered her most was the gossip about Alpha Delta being involved. Because if Alpha Delta was involved, then Daniel had to be. And if Daniel knew something and wasn't talking, then he wasn't the guy she thought he was—and liked.

"Daniel," she thought aloud wistfully.

"You called?" a voice said.

Liz looked up to see Daniel peering over the top of her partition. Part of her wanted to ask him straight out—are you involved in this thing? What do you know?

But she chickened out because she didn't want him to think she was accusing him. Still, she knew it was important to find out the truth.

"Working hard?" he asked.

Liz rolled her eyes. "Hardly working."

"I know what you mean. Is it Tim?"

Liz threw down her pencil. "Is it ever. How about a cup of coffee? Mine's cold."

Daniel tried to smile. "How about three?"

Downstairs, in the Cave, they took a private corner table, next to a mural of a dragon blowing fire.

Liz decided to dive right in. "How's everyone at Alpha Delt?"

Daniel seemed to wince at the mention of his frat brothers. "As well as can be expected. It's no fun to lose one of your own."

"*Lose* one of your own?" Liz inquired.

Daniel acted annoyed. "You know what I mean. We're all bummed about Tim. Especially the pledges."

Liz cocked her head. "Why the pledges especially?"

Daniel seemed caught off guard. He shrugged. "Why not?"

They both sipped their coffee in silence. Liz

could tell Daniel was uncomfortable. He wouldn't meet her eye. It was as if they had had a fight, but without an argument. Now she really wanted to know what this was all about.

"So what do you think Tim was doing out by the Coop anyway," Liz probed.

Daniel pushed away his coffee and eyed her suspiciously. "Did Nancy put you up to all this questioning?"

"Nancy?" Liz asked. "What makes you think Nancy told me to ask you anything?"

Daniel only shrugged. "Forget I ever said it," he mumbled.

"Really, Daniel," Liz insisted. "What do you mean?"

Still, he wouldn't say a thing.

Liz leaned on the slate table and sullenly watched the other architecture students milling around, working out drawings on napkins.

She was torn. She didn't want to push Daniel. But she was positive there was something he wasn't telling her. And if he was as upset about Tim as he said he was, why wouldn't he do everything he could to help him?

What are you not telling me! Liz wanted to ask. What are you hiding?

"So, where did you say you're taking me?" Jake asked as Nancy strode in front of him toward fraternity row.

"I didn't," Nancy replied jokingly.

"That's right, all I got was an urgent 'I have to show you something,'" he said.

Nancy grinned. When she'd spotted Jake on campus, she had a sudden urge to be with him. To show him what she'd discovered at the Coop. At least that was her excuse.

But it didn't hurt that grabbing him by the arm and dragging him away was fun all on its own. Especially since he actually came with her.

"If you'd rather run back to the *Times* office to type up the notes in your interview with the Greek Life Committee—" she began.

"Which I'm sure you can imagine was a bust," Jake interrupted. "Talking to them—especially about drinking on campus—is like talking to a brick wall."

Jake was still working on the story of Tim's accident and told Nancy that he had gone to the Greek Life Committee to get some comments about the problem of out-of-control drinking at frat parties.

"So do you want me to guess where we're going, or is this a treasure hunt?" Jake asked.

"You could guess," Nancy said. "But I wouldn't bother. You'd never get it."

Jake stopped and narrowed his eyes. "You underestimate me," he protested.

"I don't think so," Nancy said, smiling. He *was* cute, she thought.

"And what does that mean?" Jake asked defensively.

Nancy started walking again. She spied the Alpha Delta house at the top of the hill and quickened her pace. "It means whatever you want it to mean," she said flippantly.

Nancy saw Jake's brown eyes flash his annoyance, and she smiled. You're cute, she wanted to say. But she wouldn't have wanted him to take it the wrong way.

And which way was that? Nancy grilled herself. She didn't know. She hadn't thought much about it. But something deep in her brain, some tiny voice, warned her that maybe she should.

Alpha Delta was just above them now. Nancy led Jake off to the right, toward the Coop.

"I'm sorry I couldn't go with you yesterday morning," Nancy said. "I really had to tell Kara."

"I understand," Jake replied.

"But I wouldn't pick her over you in *every* situation," Nancy said, watching Jake for his reaction.

Jake smiled. "That's nice to know," he said.

There was an awkward silence, until Nancy cleared her throat.

"I went to see Tim at the hospital again this morning," she said.

"The doctor I interviewed said Tim drank too much," Jake said. "It's as simple as that."

Nancy shook her head. "Don't believe everything you hear. Tim didn't drink," she explained.

"Yeah, I heard that, too," Jake said, "but you never know."

Nancy looked up at the Coop. "I think this story will be full of surprises," she said suggestively. "But not the surprises you think."

"Is that why you brought me here?"

Nancy pointed up to the Coop's upper windows.

"Look at that window and tell me what you see," Nancy prodded.

Jake looked up, then back down at Nancy, an amused expression on his face.

"Do you see it?" Nancy asked impatiently. "Do you understand what it means?"

Jake's brow furrowed, and when he spoke, Nancy could hear he was struggling not to laugh.

"Have you spoken to it?" Jake asked, his voice quivering. "Do you think it saw something?"

"What?" Nancy asked, confused. "Spoken to what? I'm talking about what's inside the Coop!"

Nancy glanced up at the window, and when she saw what was there, her arm fell to her side. A squirrel with a nut in its mouth was wriggling out of the Coop through the broken window. The unrepaired broken window. No cardboard, no tape. Nothing left to prove that anyone had been inside except a squirrel storing food for the winter.

Nancy slapped her forehead. "That's pretty funny," she said, laughing at herself. "You must think I'm really weird."

Jake shrugged and grinned. "I'm waiting for you to change my mind."

Nancy turned quickly toward the frat house just as an upstairs curtain stirred, and a figure stepped back from the window.

"What's wrong?" Jake asked. "You look like you've seen a ghost."

I think I have, Nancy thought. "I was wrong to bring you here," she said sadly.

"Why?"

"I can't tell you now. There's nothing definite."

"But I don't need 'definite,' " Jake insisted. "Just tell me your theory. We'll get to the definite stuff later."

Nancy could tell Jake was dying of frustration, but she just shook her head. It was too important to leave to guesswork. She was sure that that window had been taped from the inside.

And if that's true, she thought, then Daniel lied to me about the building being shut down. Why?

"There has to be a way inside," she murmured.

"Inside what?" Jake asked excitedly.

"I'm really sorry, Jake," Nancy said.

She wanted to tell him. But it wouldn't be right.

Nancy peered hard at the Coop, trying unsuccessfully to see much through the vines and ivy.

Whatever it took, she had to find a way in.

Jake stood at the corner, watching Nancy head across the quad, back to her dorm.

"I know you're keeping something from me,"

he said in her direction. But she was already out of earshot.

He'd tried everything to pry Nancy's secret from her, but she wasn't budging.

"You're onto something about Tim Downing's accident," he murmured. "I know it. I can feel it."

But he also knew he'd have to wait until she was ready to trust him with what she knew or thought she knew.

But as he turned and headed for the newspaper office, he felt hurt and frustrated. Not only as a reporter, but as something more.

Brian was taking the stairs up to his room two at a time. The afternoon rehearsal for *Grease!* had been about to start at Hewlitt Auditorium when Brian realized he'd forgotten his script. He didn't really need it anymore, but it was like his security blanket.

Brian unlocked his door, grabbed the script on his desk, and sprinted back across campus back to the auditorium.

The stage lights were on. The chorus had taken their places for a test run of the finale. Brian slipped in beside Bess.

"Where have you been?" she whispered out of the side of her mouth. "I was getting worried about you."

Brian winked. "My dorm's not around the corner—unlike some people's," he scolded her kiddingly.

The rehearsal pianist's fingers ran down the keyboard, filling the auditorium with beautiful chords. Brian took a deep breath, chasing away the chills of performance nerves. He felt ready, excited to sing his heart out.

Smiling, he flipped open his script to glance through it before tossing it aside. His face reddened, and his eyes burned with anger as he saw that someone had scrawled in red pen all over the first page: "Come out, come out wherever you are—or pay for the Piper's brand-new car!"

Stunned, Brian dropped the script. Everyone looked at him. He swept it up and stumbled off toward the wings.

Behind him, he could hear everyone start to sing.

"Looking for me?" Nancy asked as she walked into the suite. Liz was about to knock on Nancy's door.

"Am I ever," Liz said anxiously.

Nancy led her in.

"Oh, hi, Kara."

Kara smiled sadly.

When she saw the sparkle was gone from Kara's eyes, Nancy gave her a hug.

"How's he doing?" Liz asked.

Kara shrugged. "No change, really. Frank located his parents, and they arrived a little while ago. I didn't think I should butt in, so I came back to take a nap."

"I'm sure they wouldn't mind if you were there," Nancy said.

Kara smiled slightly. "You're just cheering me up."

"But it's working," Liz said. "Right?"

Kara laughed despite herself. "Well, maybe I should get back there. See you later."

After Kara left, Nancy dropped onto her bed and sighed. "It's awful seeing her so sad," she said.

"I wanted to tell you about something," Liz said, taking Kara's chair. "It might have something to do with Tim's accident. Or it might not, I'm so confused, I can't keep anything straight anymore."

Nancy nodded. "I know what you mean."

"I had a strange conversation with Daniel a little while ago. I think he knows something."

"Really?" Nancy sat up. "What makes you think so?"

"Well, he brought up your name, for one. He said you've been hassling him with questions about the Coop. But I didn't think that sounded like you. I just thought he was being oversensitive." She looked at Nancy worriedly and dropped her voice. "I'd really hate it if he was involved in Tim's problem."

Nancy sighed. "Unfortunately, I think he might be, Liz. I overheard him and Tim talking the other night at the party. Daniel had said something about 'select,' and about some kind of walk."

"But Daniel told me he had to be in studio all night after the party!" Liz exclaimed.

"That's what he told Tim, too. But then when Kara and I were in Tim's room, I picked up a piece of paper that had 'You have been selected,' written on it."

" 'Select,' hmmm? Like you heard him and Daniel talking about?"

Nancy nodded. "I can't be positive, of course, but I think so. Also, before that, the nurse at the clinic handed us a medallion Tim had been wearing. It had an *S* inscribed on it."

Liz cocked her head. "Was it silver and heavy and old looking?"

"Yes!" Nancy cried. "You saw it?"

"Daniel has one, too. But he told me it was a high school graduation present from his parents, and that the *S* stood for *success*. Come to think of it, though, I haven't seen him wear it the last couple of days."

"You really think that *S* stood for *success*?" Nancy asked dubiously.

Liz shook her head. "That medallion would have been a really weird gift from a parent," she surmised.

"That's what I think," Nancy said. "I think that Tim was wearing Daniel's medallion that night— but why?"

Nancy and Liz were quiet for a minute. Finally Nancy turned to Liz. "You said Daniel was at the studio that night. And that's where he told Tim he'd be . . ."

Liz picked up the thought. "So whatever happened, Daniel probably wasn't involved?" she asked hopefully.

"Not physically," Nancy said thoughtfully. "But he knows something. I'm sure of it."

Liz frowned. "Unfortunately, the Alpha Delts' loyalty to one another is well-known. I heard they take a secrecy oath. The frat has nationwide connections, and if you break the oath, it can come back to haunt you."

Nancy shuddered. It's so strange that a college fraternity could have that much power, she thought.

"But maybe we don't need to ask Daniel to reveal any secrets," Nancy said. "At least not directly."

Liz leaned forward, listening as Nancy told her about the taped window at the Coop, even though the Alpha Delts claimed it had been shut up tight for twenty years.

"You think the Coop was involved with Tim's accident," Liz concluded.

"I'm sure of it," Nancy said firmly. "But I can't prove it unless we get inside. Which, unfortunately, we can't."

"Because we don't know how to," Liz said distractedly.

"Right. If we only knew a way to get in."

"If we could only get our hands on the architectural plans, you mean?" Liz asked, smiling.

Nancy nodded.

Liz got up. "I might have just the thing for that little problem," she said. "Meet me in front of Rand Hall in an hour?"

Nancy winced. "I have to give my father and his new girlfriend a campus tour today. How about tonight?"

Liz nodded. "Nine o'clock?"

Nancy stood up. "Nine sharp," she said, grinning.

Bess pushed through the doors of Brian's dorm and out into the early evening air. Casey was standing there with Charley. "So, did you find Brian?" Casey asked.

Bess shook her head. "You?"

"Nope," Casey said. "We looked all over. And I'm really worried about him."

"He must have had the worst case of stage fright ever," Charley commented.

"It wasn't stage fright," Bess replied. "Brian loves being onstage. He's a natural—"

"Unfortunately, if he misses one more rehearsal, he's in danger of losing his part," Casey said.

"We've been chasing around after Brian for hours," Charley said. "And I haven't eaten since this morning. When I came out to see you, Case,

I didn't think following you around would be so hard. I'm exhausted—and starved!"

Casey grinned. "You can't believe college is such hard work, can you?"

"It makes Hollywood seem like a piece of cake."

"It does," Casey said. "Believe me, it does."

CHAPTER 10

Liz was standing outside Rand Hall anxiously waiting for Nancy. In the distance, she could hear live music from the Underground. Straining her eyes to see in the dark, Liz finally saw a figure hurry toward her.

"Nancy." Liz breathed a sigh of relief. "I was getting worried that Daniel would come by and I wouldn't know how to explain what we were up to. Come on inside."

"Sorry I'm late," Nancy said apologetically.

"Wow!" Nancy whistled as Liz led her from the stairway into the vast second-floor studio of Rand Hall. Remembering what it looked like to her the first time she walked in made Liz laugh in sympathy.

"It is pretty crazy, isn't it?" she asked, gazing around. The walls and partitions everywhere made the space look like a huge maze. There were scraps of paper with plans and drawings tacked up on every available surface.

There were enlarged photocopies of funny cartoons, messages and silly notes, party hats, goggles, magazine covers, and even a rubber rat stuck onto one of the columns with a big tack. The rule was, if you could name it, it was probably on a wall somewhere in Rand.

"I can't believe you actually get work done here," Nancy said in amazement.

"It's true that things get a little silly in studio," Liz admitted. "But that's just because we spend so much time here and work so hard. If we didn't find a way to blow off steam we'd all go crazy. Anyway," Liz continued as she led Nancy around a few more narrow corners, "here we are!"

Nancy looked at the tight little cubicle with the drawing table and swing-arm lamp and shook her head. "I'm impressed. This almost feels like a space for a job or something."

"It seems like that sometimes," Liz admitted. "It's hard to remember there's a whole university full of students out there having lives, which is why it's nice to get out of here to go to a party or something. . . ." Liz trailed off and grimaced, as she remembered her last party.

Nancy reached out and squeezed her shoulder.

"Anyway," Liz continued, getting out a roll of drawings, "I'd rather go somewhere else to look at these. Daniel's table is on this floor, too. I'd rather not have him see us. We'll stop by so I can leave him a note. That way he won't come looking for me."

They stopped in front of Daniel's desk. As always, Liz was amazed at how neat Daniel kept his space. Most architecture students were total slobs.

"Let me just get a scrap of paper," Liz muttered, wishing that Daniel was more of a slob. She pulled open a few drawers until she found one with paper. She reached in to pull a sheet out, but caught her hand and ended up pulling a whole wad of stuff from the drawer. Papers spilled everywhere onto the floor.

Liz sighed as she stooped to put everything back, but when her hand fell on a familiar roll of paper, she gasped. She stood straight and unrolled it, and found herself staring at a plan for the Alpha Delta house. But this was no copy, like the ones she'd made.

This was an original, and in the corner, she saw a faint "#12" marked in pencil—the same drawing the attendant in the archives had said was missing.

Liz could feel Nancy tugging on her sleeve. "Liz, what is it?"

"I'll tell you," Liz muttered quickly, "but we've got to get out of here. Now!"

Nancy picked up the rest of the papers while Liz quickly scrawled a note for Daniel. Then Liz grabbed Nancy by the arm and led her back toward the stairway.

What's so special about drawing number #12? Liz was dying to know. Whatever it is, we're about to find out, she thought as she tucked plan #12 in with her other papers and closed the drawer.

"Okay, your turn, Bess," Holly Thornton said pleasantly.

Bess, Eileen, and the other ten pledges in their pledge class were sitting in the middle of the floor of the Kappa living room with the other Kappa sisters standing around them.

"That's right," Soozie Beckerman said, chuckling. "Time for you to open up, Bess, and remember, this is a sign of loyalty to the house. If you don't want to share something with us, we'll have to wonder whether you really want to be a Kappa or not."

"So what should we ask her?" another Kappa asked.

"Hmm," Soozie pondered. "How about that guy she hangs out with," Soozie said. "What's his name? The cute blond?"

"Brian?" Bess asked. "You want to know about Brian?"

"Sure," Soozie replied. "Tell us everything about you and Brian—all the good gossipy bits, and don't leave anything out."

"But—but," Bess stammered, "there's nothing to tell. I mean, he's just a friend."

"Well," Soozie pressed, "do you have a crush on him? Does he have a crush on you? Is it destined to be unrequited love, or what? Come on, Bess, we want to be entertained, and 'just a friend' is not very entertaining."

"But he really is," Bess said quickly. "I mean, I had a crush on him when we first met, but then—" Bess stopped herself. She'd been about to tell them Brian's secret! She couldn't do that, no matter what they asked.

"But then?" Soozie prompted anxiously.

"But then we decided just to be friends," Bess said weakly.

"Very boring story," Soozie said. "I give it a D-plus."

"It's not *that* bad," Holly challenged her. "I give it a B."

"Okay, *maybe* a C-minus," Soozie gave in.

"Did you have a bad date or something?" one of the Kappa sisters asked.

"No," Bess replied.

"So how about you plan to *go* on a bad date with him?" Soozie said. "Then you can tell us all about it."

"Soozie!" Holly said. "Cut it out. You don't have to be so mean."

"But we'll never go on a date," Bess went on. "I just don't feel anything for him like that."

"No way, Bess," another Kappa sister said.

"How could you not feel anything. He's too cute!"

"Maybe it's you who's the Ice Princess and not that awful roommate of yours," Soozie wondered out loud.

"That's not it," Bess said slowly, trying desperately to think of a way out of the conversation. "It's just that he's not my type, that's all—"

"The only way he wouldn't be *my* type is if he were gay," another sister said.

Bess couldn't hide her mortified reaction. "Don't say that," she cried loudly.

"Jeez, I was just joking," the sister replied.

"But you weren't, Bess," Soozie said, studying her thoughtfully. "Were you?"

Bess couldn't think of an answer. She certainly wasn't going to tell them it was all true, but she also couldn't make herself lie about it.

"Okay, okay," Holly's voice said impatiently. "That's enough of that, Soozie. Time to move on to the next pledge."

Bess listened as the Kappa sisters started grilling Eileen about *her* life. Why were the only secrets juicy enough to share the ones that had to do with guys? Bess thought bitterly. Because, an inner voice reminded her sadly, when a girl shares her secrets about a guy, it's a sign of trust.

Again, Bess thought of George, and how they hadn't really talked since that morning at the Souvlaki House. George hadn't trusted Bess enough to tell her about Will until afterward. Which meant she hadn't really cared about, or wanted, Bess's advice.

Bess really missed George. Never in a million years did she think she'd be telling a roomful of almost strangers more about herself than she told her closest cousin.

But she never thought her closest cousin would think she wasn't worth talking to either.

"Did you say Casey Fontaine is interested in Kappa?" Soozie asked, snapping Bess from her gloomy thoughts in an instant.

"Well," Eileen hedged, "she did say that, right, Bess?"

"When we were at the Alpha Delt party," Bess confirmed. "She said she was thinking about joining."

"Well, she shouldn't just think about it," Soozie said eagerly. "And it's up to you guys to convince her to join."

As Bess and the other pledges rose wearily to their feet, Soozie and some of the Kappa sisters were huddled together whispering. Then Soozie stood back up and said good night to all of them.

"Tonight was a very educational night. I learned a lot," Soozie added with a grin as the girls began filing out of the room.

"Especially from you, Bess," Soozie said quietly.

Bess stopped, her heart missing a beat.

"About the Casey situation, of course," Soozie continued.

"Right," Bess agreed, breathing a sigh of relief.

"And your poor friend Brian," Soozie said with a smirk. "What a *shame,* don't you think?"

Bess tried not to think about what she meant, or worry about it, but she couldn't help it. If Bess had unwittingly given away Brian's secret, he would be very hurt.

Please don't be as interested as you seem, Soozie, Bess silently begged her. And please don't let it get around.

"Okay, so let's see it," Nancy said, snapping on the fluorescent bar underneath the light table in the photography studio of the Fine Arts building. The photographer from the *Wilder Times* was the monitor in charge of studio supplies, and Nancy had been able to talk him into opening the studio to let them use the table to check out the plans.

Liz dropped all the drawings onto the table. The tight curls of paper went rolling everywhere.

"One at a time, then," Nancy suggested.

"But let's look at this one first," Liz said, spreading out the brittle piece of paper she'd taken from Daniel's desk. "This is an original plan," Liz added. "Isn't it cool?"

"It is cool," Nancy admitted. Whoever had drawn the plans was quite an artist and had put a lot of time and effort into it. There were all sorts of curlicues and flourishes as if the drawing were a work of art and not just a plan for a building. As Nancy scanned the drawing, she noticed faint black writing along one side. She peered closer and read, "You have been selected."

"Look at this!" Nancy exclaimed, remembering the note she saw in Tim's room. "There's no way this could be a coincidence."

"It's that word again," Liz murmured, as she read what Nancy had found.

"This *selected* thing must be what Daniel and Tim were talking about at the party," Nancy said firmly.

"And if Daniel had this, he already knew what it meant," Liz agreed.

"This was in Daniel's desk?" Nancy mused.

"For at least a year," Liz nodded.

"So maybe the *S* on his medallion really stands for *select*," Nancy thought aloud. "And if Daniel was 'selected,' and Tim was 'selected,' then maybe it wasn't Daniel's medallion Tim had."

"He had his own?" Liz guessed.

Nancy nodded. A picture of Chip Booth standing in the doorway of the secret meeting room flashed into Nancy's mind along with Tim's comment about rush pranks and how Chip would make sure they were carried out, with a vengeance.

If Tim's accident was the result of fraternity hazing, Chip Booth would have to have known about it, Nancy reasoned.

While Nancy was thinking, Liz laid out another

drawing—this one a floor plan of the Coop, which wasn't originally called that. On the top of the drawing was precise script: "The Annex."

"Mmm, I wonder when it got the name the Coop?" Liz said quietly as if reading Nancy's mind.

As Nancy continued to scan the drawing, she noticed an intricate little curlicue like those on drawing number 12.

"Liz," Nancy said, pointing at the funny little marking. "What is that? It doesn't look like anything else on the plan."

Liz bent over and peered closely at it. Nancy heard her mutter something and then shake her head.

"I'm not sure, exactly," Liz admitted.

Nancy unrolled some of the other drawings and tried to find similar markings on them. There were none.

"Maybe it was a mistake," Liz suggested.

"Maybe," Nancy agreed, but she had a feeling it was more important. Finally she went back to the drawing they'd taken from Daniel's desk.

"What part of the house is this again?" Nancy asked as she scanned the drawing closely.

"It's the basement," Liz replied.

"Look!" Nancy said, suddenly excited as her finger came to rest on something. "Here it is again. It's that same mark, isn't it?"

Liz put the two drawings side by side and studied them carefully.

"It definitely is," Liz agreed. "It looks like a door, but this funny little mark covers it up."

"Kind of like a secret door?" Nancy said. She'd felt that the two buildings could be connected somehow; otherwise, how else could anyone have gotten into the Coop.

"A secret door," Liz mused, staring intently at the drawings. "Perhaps," she said. "But I don't think it's the door that's supposed to be a secret."

"What do you mean?" Nancy asked excitedly.

"I think it's what *connects* the doors that's meant to be hidden," Liz replied. "There's a passageway or something there," she explained. "And the door is in this room." Liz put her finger down onto a small square on the drawing.

"Well," Nancy said, "I guess we'll just have to find out whose room that is, won't we?"

CHAPTER 11

When Nancy arrived at Java Joe's the next morning, she stood in the little vestibule and laughed at the sight of her father and Avery, surrounded by tables of chattering students. She'd wanted to give her father a taste of college life, but maybe Java Joe's at ten on a Saturday morning was overkill.

"Sorry I'm late," Nancy said, sliding into the booth opposite them. "And I hope this place is okay."

Avery was beaming. "I *love* it!" she said. Avery leaned across the table and lowered her voice conspiratorially. "It reminds me of my college boyfriend. We used to come to a place just like this every Sunday morning for breakfast."

"What did you do last night?" Nancy asked.

Avery squeezed Carson's arm. "Your father

took me to the movies. The film was so awful, it was wonderful!"

Carson Drew laughed his deep, throaty laugh. "I'll definitely agree with that!"

Nancy laughed along with her father. "Isn't college great?" she asked.

"You certainly made a wonderful choice," Carson said.

Out of the corner of her eye, Nancy saw George and Bess barreling through the door. "Brace yourselves," she warned.

"Mr. Drew!" Bess shouted.

Carson got to his feet and embraced both of Nancy's friends in the aisle.

"And you must be Avery," Bess said, holding out her hand.

"So you're Bess," Avery replied.

"That's me," Bess said. "And it's great to meet you!"

George and Bess wedged into Nancy's side of the booth.

"I see what you mean," Avery said.

Nancy threw her an inquiring look.

"Carson told me that you three were the most impressive and beautiful group of young women he'd ever met. And the most loyal friends. I can see he didn't exaggerate one tiny bit."

Nancy glanced at Bess to see if she'd finally forgiven George. Bess was slightly flushed, and Nancy knew when Bess was really happy, or just trying to be happy. And right now, Bess was still trying.

"I was hoping I would get to see all of you," Carson was saying. "The last month, I've felt like I have three daughters in college."

The five of them ordered omelettes and toast and home fries and orange juice and coffee. Carson made Bess and George run through each of their class schedules and tell him about every course.

After a few minutes, Avery sat back and scanned the debris in front of them. "Boy, this table looks like a battlefield!"

"So what are everybody's plans for today?" Carson asked.

"I'm meeting Will at the library to study," George said.

Nancy snorted. "And I bet you'll get lots of work done."

"Ah, yes, Mr. Blackfeather. He seemed terrific, George," Carson said.

"Uh-oh, girls, watch out"—Avery grinned—"here comes Father."

"Don't you love him, Mr. Drew?" Bess asked excitedly. "Nancy and I think he's the greatest."

George was beaming. "You do? You mean it?"

Bess nodded eagerly, which made Nancy wonder if Bess was coming around.

"Well, from just the short meeting we had yesterday, I'd say I have no choice but to approve," Carson said.

"What about you, Bess?" Avery asked. "Anybody special?"

Bess sighed. "The stage is my romance," she said in a mock British accent, fanning herself with her ketchup-stained napkin.

Everyone at the table broke up. "Nancy told me all about it. I can't wait to come see your debut," Carson said.

"Uh-oh, I have to get to the newspaper in a few minutes," Nancy cut in, looking at her watch. "I have some work to get done to meet a deadline. And I need to check on a story Jake is working on."

"Jake. That's the young man you mentioned the other day," Carson said.

"The one you think is such a wonderful writer," Avery added.

"That's the second time you've brought up this Jake. There wouldn't be any interest in him other than professional, would there?" Carson probed.

Nancy was blushing. She could tell there was something else behind her father's question. Ned.

Nancy had told her father about the break-up, but they hadn't really had a conversation about it. She knew he was interested, and right now he was looking at her as if he wanted to know she was okay.

"Jake's just a friend," Nancy said, squeezing her father's arm. "Which is fine, right now."

"Okay," Carson replied. "But you know I'm here any time you want to talk."

"I know that," Nancy replied.

"What about tonight?" Carson asked.

"I can't—there's a party at Alpha Delt I have to go to," Nancy said sadly.

Carson raised an eyebrow. He seemed ready to say something more when Avery held up her hands. "Say no more. A college woman's got to have her parties. Carson, you can take me to a lovely romantic dinner. Candles, soft music, a little dancing."

Nancy's father was beaming at her. Nancy could see that her father would like nothing more.

"Oh, and Nancy, I have that little gift for you in the trunk of my car," Carson said.

"It's a computer," Nancy told Bess and George. "Thanks, Dad. Now I can enter the twentieth century."

They made a plan to meet for brunch the next morning after Carson and Avery checked out of their hotel.

Outside, Bess and George went one way, and Nancy the other, toward the newspaper.

While she was walking, she thought of her father's question about Jake.

Well, I *have* been thinking more and more about Jake lately, she confessed to herself. And I'm not sure that calling him a friend is really the truth.

Nancy knew that she didn't have to tell Jake about what she'd learned with Liz last night about the Alpha Delt house and the Coop, but she wanted him to know. She'd tell him as soon as possible.

Brian opened his eyes as the phone rang. He glanced at the clock. It was ten. He'd rarely slept that late before. He prided himself on being an early riser.

But now his shades were drawn, and he ducked back under his blanket to block out the sound of the phone ringing.

"It's that creep," Brian whispered, "that cruel idiot."

He couldn't finish the thought. Who was doing this to him? He had no idea. But even scarier, whoever it was knew him. He knew Brian's father was a politician, vulnerable to scandal. He knew Brian's deepest secrets, his emotional bruises.

The phone kept ringing.

"Go away!" Brian cried.

Finally the answering machine picked up and Brian held his breath as he heard his own voice asking the caller to please leave a message.

Then the long beep.

Brian squeezed his eyes tight, afraid to hear the voice.

"Hi, Brian. It's Mom," the voice said. "Your father and I would like to know when we should come to see your play. We'd like to talk it over with you, honey. Just a quick call, when you have a sec. 'Bye for now!"

Brian listened to the click, and then the machine shutting off. He couldn't even pick up the phone and talk to his own mother.

This is ruining my life! Brian thought.

Then the horrifying thought struck him. This could get a whole lot worse, and probably would.

As Nancy stepped through the door to the *Wilder Times* office, she heard computer keyboards clicking in many of the cubicles. The smell of fresh-brewed coffee was in the air, which meant that Jake was probably around. But where? His desk, usually covered with paper, pizza boxes, and empty coffee cups, was cleared off, and Jake was nowhere in sight.

She walked toward her cubicle and heard someone on her computer. She stepped around the partition and found Jake typing away, a pencil behind his ear.

"Make yourself at home," Nancy said, smiling.

"Thanks," Jake said, not taking his eyes from the screen. "I will."

"Does this mean that I get to move to your desk?" Nancy asked tongue-in-cheek.

Jake shook his head. "I just wanted a change of scenery."

Nancy peered over his shoulder. "What are you working on?"

"I'm typing up my notes on the Tim Downing thing," he replied, swiveling back toward her.

Nancy sat on the edge of the desk and wondered whether her motives for sharing the information were those of a reporter, or whether there was another reason she wanted to see Jake.

He was peering at her with his rich brown eyes, his mouth fixed in a half-smile. "Are you trying to say something?" he asked.

"Um," Nancy said.

Jake nodded. *"Really.* Wait a sec, let me get that down." He swiveled back to his computer and typed two letters with his index finger. "Um," he repeated. "There. Excellent. Now, was there anything else?"

Nancy broke up. She loved the way he made her laugh.

"I'm sorry, Jake. I really am. Actually, there is something. Remember how I dragged you over to the Coop?"

"How could I forget? Did you ever track down that furry little witness?"

Nancy blushed. "I was acting pretty dumb, huh?"

Jake shrugged, but Nancy could tell he was holding back another zinger.

"Actually," she said, "I thought I'd let you in on a little secret."

Jake leaned forward. "I *love* secrets."

"Well, I've been working on this theory that there's some connection between the Coop and

142

what happened to Tim Downing. I think the Alpha Delts are still using the Coop."

"But it's been shut up for twenty years," Jake said.

"That's the point," Nancy replied. "They don't want anyone to know how to get in or that they do get in. But a friend and I may have found the way."

"Let's go!" Jake said enthusiastically.

"Hold on a minute." Nancy laughed, putting her hand on Jake's shoulder. "What are you going to do? Run over there with your notebook and say, 'Take me to your secret passage'?"

"Well," Jake said, "I guess not. So I take it you have a plan?"

Nancy nodded. "My friend managed to get me an invitation to the Alpha Delt dance tonight."

"Your plan is a date?" Jake asked.

"Yes," Nancy teased, "a date named Liz."

"Good," Jake said quickly. "Okay, go on."

"That's it," Nancy replied.

Jake was nodding. "I see. So you mingle, I find the secret passageway, then . . ."

"Unfortunately, the invitation is only for one." Nancy grinned.

"Oh, I get it," Jake cried, understanding lighting his eyes. "*You* mingle, then *you* find the secret passageway, right? Boy, and to think you called me the star reporter. Empty flattery, I guess."

Nancy laughed. "Liz and I thought that in the

confusion of the party, we could slip away unnoticed," she explained.

Jake looked at her meaningfully. "I don't think *you* could go *anywhere* unnoticed," he said.

Nancy smiled. "That was sweet," she said quietly.

"Well, just so you know. In the future, *my* invitations are always for *two*," Jake said.

"I can't wait," Nancy answered, excited that he'd sort of asked her out, and she'd sort of said yes.

"You mean that?" he asked.

Nancy nodded. "As long as it's not for tonight."

Jake walked back to his desk with a full cup of coffee, relieved that Nancy had finally confided in him about her plans.

She does trust me, he realized happily. He was definitely thinking of Nancy not just as a new reporter, but also as a beautiful young woman who sent his heart racing every time she passed anywhere near.

And if she thinks I'm going to let her endanger herself and try to crack this story alone, she's crazy. She needs my experience—and connections.

"Let's see," he said, pulling out his old address book. "After a couple of years on campus, there must be a few people who owe me a favor—or three."

CHAPTER 12

Luckily Nancy was in her room when Bess stopped by late that evening. She'd been wanting to talk to Nancy since the night before, but hadn't had time.

She needed to talk to Nancy about betraying Brian's trust, but she didn't know how to do it without betraying it again! She couldn't tell the story to Nancy if she didn't also tell her that Brian was gay. But if she didn't talk to someone about it soon, Bess was sure her head would explode! Bess was sure that Nancy would be able to straighten it all out.

"Nan?" Bess called after knocking on Nancy's door. "Are you there?"

"Bess?" Nancy's muffled voice replied. "Come in! I'm here," she continued as Bess slipped into her room, "but only for another ten minutes or so. I'm on my way to a dance at Alpha Delt."

"Who are you going with?" Bess asked, surprised as she watched Nancy do a pretty good imitation of Kara plowing through a closet. As far as Bess knew, Nancy wasn't dating anyone. Unless, of course, this was another piece of news Bess would be the last to hear.

"I'm not going with a guy," Nancy admitted, surfacing from the closet. "But I wangled an invitation anyway, and I'm going with Liz. So," Nancy began, as she brushed her reddish blond hair back to put it into a soft chignon, "what's up with you? Any plans?"

"No plans," Bess admitted. "I just came to talk. By the way, it was great seeing your dad this morning," Bess said. "And Avery seems really nice."

"Yeah," Nancy agreed, pausing long enough to smile. "She really does. To be honest, I still feel a little funny seeing Dad with a girlfriend," Nancy said softly. "But I really like Avery."

"It has been a long time since your mom died, Nancy," Bess said. "And sometimes a real person can be just as nice as a memory."

Nancy stopped what she was doing and hugged Bess. "Thanks. That was a lovely thing to say," she said. Letting go of her friend, Nancy pulled on a yellow- and black-flowered dress that flared gently around her knees.

Before Bess could respond, the door opened and Nancy's suitemate Liz stood there, wearing her usual black, this time in the form of loose pants and a vest.

"Now, don't say a word!" Liz joked, holding up her hand. "Black has always been and always will be *the* glamorous and sophisticated color for evening wear."

"And funerals," Nancy said mockingly.

"Right," Liz agreed in stride. "I'll amend that to tasteful and correct in *all* social situations. Anyway, are you ready? We've got to get going."

Bess watched as Nancy grabbed her bag and a jacket.

"I'm sorry for running out on you like this, Bess," she said apologetically. "But thanks for stopping by. And for what you said before." Nancy gave her a quick squeeze. "I really feel a lot better."

But I don't, Bess wanted to say as the last of Nancy's yellow-and-black dress fluttered out the door. Bess sighed. She'd come to get help, not to give it.

"Well," Bess muttered to herself. "Since I'm here, I may as well do something productive."

She got up and went out into the hall to knock on Casey's door. Perhaps now was a good time to find out if Casey really was interested in joining Kappa. The sisters would be happy to hear if she was, and Bess didn't mind doing them this favor. At least the Kappas want to hear what I have to say, Bess thought. Which is more than my friends have been doing lately.

But when Casey answered her door, Bess could see right away that her mind wasn't on Kappa. Casey's red hair was mussed, and her eyes were a little red. Bess could see Charley Stern sitting on Casey's bed.

"I'm sorry to bother you," Bess apologized. "Maybe we can talk later."

"Oh, that's okay," Casey said. "I know I look awful, but Charley's leaving in half an hour, and all of a sudden it hit me how much I miss him, and he isn't even gone yet."

"You could still come with me," Charley teased from inside the room. "Back to the exciting, crazy, high-energy world of Hollywood."

Bess thought she saw Casey shudder before she grimaced good-naturedly. "Now all of a sudden, I feel better about staying here," Casey joked. Then she leaned over to Bess conspiratorially. "Is it possible that the Thayer Hall cafeteria staff has been slipping something into my food?"

Bess laughed at Casey's natural actress antics.

"Anyway"—Casey smiled—"can whatever you want to talk about wait? I promise next time I'll be up to hanging out."

"Of course," Bess said quickly. "I didn't mean to interrupt."

" 'Bye, Bess," Charley called. "It was nice meeting you."

"You, too," Bess almost whispered. It still gave her a little thrill to think that Charley Stern actually knew her name.

Bess stepped back as Casey closed the door of her room. Then she wandered down the short hall to the lounge. It was empty.

Of course, it's Saturday night, Bess thought. And everyone else in the world has something fun to do. Suddenly Bess saw the lounge phone. She had such an urge to call George—to rent a movie and order pizza. To just hang out together talking the way they used to.

"Dream on, Bess," she told herself softly as she left and closed the door behind her. "George has a wonderful guy now, and a real relationship. She doesn't have time for you anymore."

At the door to Alpha Delta, Liz pulled out her two squares of pink paper with the house stamp on them. An Alpha Delta brother marked a small black *X* on the back of her hand, and then Nancy's.

"Thank goodness it doesn't clash with my outfit," Liz joked as she and Nancy pushed their way inside. Loud music was playing and a crowd of people were dancing at the far end of the huge entrance hall. Everyone, dressed up and laughing, was there to party and have a good time.

But *we're* here for something else, Liz reminded herself, feeling the nervousness rise in her stomach. She still wasn't sure how it would all work out, but Nancy seemed confident, so Liz just shrugged and plunged into the crowd. In a few seconds, Daniel had found them.

"I was on the stairs watching for you two." He smiled, taking Liz by the hand. "You look wonderful."

Liz couldn't stop the surge that swept through her as she looked into Daniel's eyes. He was so incredibly cute.

But still in the back of her mind was the knowledge that he was hiding something about the fraternity house and about what had happened to his friend. Liz knew she was going to have trouble acting naturally, and she was already worried about what she and Nancy might find—if they found anything at all.

"Yes, I agree," Nancy said smoothly, filling Liz's silence. "Black is her color. By the way, is there anywhere we can stash our jackets? Your room, perhaps?"

"Sure," Daniel replied easily as he led them to the staircase. Liz knew she was acting weird, but her mind was whirling. Thankfully, Nancy seemed pretty calm.

"Just upstairs, down the main hall, fifth door on the left," Daniel instructed. "I'll meet you back down here." Daniel quickly searched the room for a good landmark. "Over there." He pointed to a pay phone booth shoved into a corner.

"Great!" Nancy nodded, taking Liz by the arm and pulling her up the stairs. Liz made herself smile and wave, as Daniel watched them from the main floor.

"What's wrong with me?" Liz sighed as soon as they were out of earshot. "I'm not used to this cloak and dagger stuff. I'd have been a terrible spy."

"Don't worry about it," Nancy replied, leading the way to Daniel's room. "Of course you feel weird. I do, too. I like Daniel. But if he's involved somehow . . ."

Nancy let the thought linger.

"I know," Liz said. "Let's just get this over with."

They went into Daniel's room and threw their coats on his bed.

"So," Nancy mused, "do you think we should try to get to the basement now? Probably not. We just said we'd meet Daniel back downstairs."

"Okay," Liz replied, plopping down on Daniel's bed for a minute. "Just give me a minute to find my nerve again." Liz leaned back and rolled on to her side. "Okay, let's go," she said.

Just as she was pushing herself off the bed, she saw something under Daniel's dresser. Liz reached down and pulled out a long silver chain—with a small round silver medallion engraved with the letter *S*. Liz's hand started shaking.

"Oh no," she said sadly. In a second Nancy had taken the medallion from her and pulled Liz to her feet.

As Liz followed Nancy back into the hall and downstairs, her head was spinning. It was one thing to guess that Daniel was involved and another to wonder if the medallion they'd found with Tim was his own. But now here was the proof that Daniel had been lying all along.

Liz and Nancy made their way through the crowd toward the telephone booth to meet Daniel. What will I say to him? Liz wondered. How will I act?

Then he was in front of her and her questions were answered.

"Hi," she managed to say. "Great party."

Daniel looked at her strangely. "Are you okay?" he asked, full of concern.

"Sure," she replied more easily. "Just overwhelmed by all the people. You know, after the claustrophobia of my cubicle in the studio—"

"This is definitely a different scene, but claustrophobic nonetheless," Daniel agreed, grinning. He turned to Nancy. "Can I get you something to drink?"

"Allow me," a deep voice spoke from behind them. Liz turned to see John Reed standing behind Nancy with a full glass. He reached around, almost hugging her, to put it in her hand.

"Mr. President." She smiled. "Thanks for the personal attention."

"Of course," John replied with easy charm. "I'm always attentive to anyone with an interest in my house. Especially when it's a beautiful woman."

Nancy nodded at the compliment, and Liz

wondered if she was the only one who felt the tension in the air.

Liz tried to smile as the conversation whirled on around her. She saw Daniel laughing. John, his eyebrows raised, fixed his gaze on Nancy. Liz knew she'd spoken at least a few times, because everyone had turned to her expectantly, but she couldn't remember a word of what they'd said. Finally, when Liz thought she was ready to scream, Nancy stepped over and grabbed her by the arm.

"Time for a visit to the ladies' room," Nancy explained.

"I guess that means we won't be seeing you for at least an hour," John teased, glancing at his watch.

"Oh, I'm sure we won't take that long," Nancy joked back.

"Not that long," Liz echoed.

"Well, I hope not," Daniel replied, a little curious.

Liz and Nancy turned and headed into the party, and as soon as they were lost in the crowd, they started off for the basement stairwell. From the plans, Liz knew the basement stairs were at the back of the house, and she and Nancy both glanced around quickly before heading down them.

The basement floor was mazelike with doors lining each side of every hall. They were looking for a room in the far northeast corner of the house.

"Okay," Liz said as they stopped in front of a plain wooden door. "This is the corner room, I think."

She reached out and grabbed the knob. Everything could have come to an end right there, if the door had been locked. Then she wouldn't have to find out the secret. Then she wouldn't have to find out how much Daniel knew. But the knob turned easily and Liz pushed the door open into a storage room strewn with piles of old clothes, football pads, soccer balls, bikes, and various pieces of furniture.

"We're supposed to find a secret door in here?" Nancy whispered. "Good camouflage job."

"Let's head over to the corner," Liz said boldly, stepping over all the debris and walking to a closet across the room. This time she didn't pause, but yanked open the closet door boldly. This is it! her mind cried immediately.

The closet was huge. There was a rack of old clothes on a pole, but both Liz and Nancy could see the dark empty space behind it. Nancy reached out and pushed the clothes aside. There it was. A small door.

"Okay," Liz murmured to herself. "Three times lucky." Her hand reached out for the knob. At first, she thought it was locked, but it was just old, and stiff. It jammed for a minute, but then turned easily. Liz pushed against the small wooden door and a blast of cool air rushed back at them and ruffled the hem of Nancy's dress.

"Ready?" Nancy asked, her expression serious, but her eyes shining with excitement.

"Sure," Liz replied with a shaky grin. "How about you first."

"You order first," Reva said, pushing Andy up to the counter of the Pizza Truck where two guys were taking orders from a crowd of students. The Pizza Truck was a small van that was usually parked near the freshman dorms in the evenings. Whenever kids had late-night hunger pangs, they usually took off for the Pizza Truck. And it was always a social scene.

Andy and Reva had been nominated by George and Will to run out and buy pizza for the four of them. She listened as Andy placed the order for four small pizzas.

They made their way back out of the crush around the truck and found a place to stand where they could breathe comfortably while they waited for their order. Reva looked at the crowd of red-eyed students around her and laughed.

"I guess there are more people working on a Saturday night than I thought," she admitted. "I was beginning to think I was crazy."

"Why?" Andy asked. "Because you're not out at the movies? Don't forget you're making money."

"That's true," Reva agreed, thinking of how busy she and Andy were with their brand-new consulting business. "But still, I don't think this is how I want to spend every Saturday night." Reva sighed, pushing her long black hair back from her face. "I'm not ready to give up on my social life my first semester of college."

"You don't think working with me is getting a jump on your social life?" Andy teased. Reva wasn't sure, but she thought there was a hint of a question behind Andy's joke.

"Sure," she replied trying to sound calm. "But if we spend *all* our time *working* together, I'll have to keep sharing you with other women."

"Are you suggesting we change our work habits?" Andy said, taking a step closer to her. "Cut down on the business end a little?"

Reva shrugged, wondering if Andy could hear the incredible pounding of her heart. It sounded like a cannon in her ears.

"Uh-oh, Reva," Andy said with mock terror, taking her hand in his and placing it on his own chest. "Now you've gotten me worried. Am I overworking? Can you feel a strain on my heart?"

Reva's breath caught in her throat as she felt Andy's heart beating as loudly and quickly as her own. She saw Andy's face coming closer. He was going to kiss her, she could feel it, and the feeling was amazing. Her only worry was that she would faint with excitement before his lips reached hers—

"TWO RONI, TWO VEGGIE!" a voice from the Pizza Truck screamed out to the crowd.

"Uh-oh," Andy said, pulling back. "That's ours." He paused for a moment, undecided, and then dropped Reva's hand and shrugged.

"You'd better grab them before someone else does." Reva nodded.

She watched Andy make his way to the Pizza Truck window. Another missed opportunity for romance, Reva thought. But then she smiled. At least now she knew that Andy felt the same way about her as she did about him. When Andy turned back to her and held their food over his head like a trophy, Reva just grinned. It was only a matter of time.

Nancy finally got to the end of the passageway, pushed open the door, and stepped in.

The Coop room was pristine, without a speck of dust anywhere, and obviously had been in use for a long time. In fact, Nancy realized, the Alpha Deltas had probably never stopped using it. They'd just boarded up the door and let the rumors start.

"This is incredible," Liz said breathlessly from behind her, and Nancy had to agree. There were strange banners hanging from the brick walls. On one of them, Nancy recognized the Alpha Delta crest—it was the same as the one on the front door of the main house. There were wooden chairs lining the walls of the room and a small podium across from the door they'd just come through.

Nancy walked over to it. In the back of the podium, there was a drawer, and when Nancy pulled it open she saw a tattered leather-bound notebook. The pages were old and yellowing, and as she fanned through them, Nancy saw names and dates going back over eighty years. Maybe these are all the brothers of Alpha Delta, she thought.

But then Nancy noticed something strange; for each date, for each year actually, there was only one name entered. Nancy flipped to the very last page and gasped. The last four names in the book, for the last four years, were John Reed, Chip Booth, Daniel Frederick, and Timothy Downing!

Nancy peered closely and saw that the date next to Tim's signature was only three nights ago—the night of his accident.

"Wow." Nancy closed the notebook. "I wonder what this is all about." Nancy was about to put the notebook back when she saw a marking on the cover, in the lower right hand corner. She ran her fingers over it, and peered closely. It was a small embossed *S*.

"The Select," Nancy murmured as the notebook suddenly clarified something for her. Now she knew that the Select *did* have something to do with Alpha Delta, but it wasn't the entire fraternity; just one brother in every class. And Tim was this year's selected student.

But why would a fraternity do that? Nancy wondered. Why would they risk hurting one of their own? She shook her head sadly.

"Hey, Nance," she heard Liz whisper from behind her. "Look at this."

Nancy hurried over and found Liz standing next to a small trunk. She'd pried up the lid and was gazing inside it, shaking her head. Nancy looked down and saw a bundled up sweatshirt. Nancy reached down to pull it out, and when she did, two bottles fell out of it and clattered to the bottom of the trunk. Vodka and tequila, and both of the bottles were empty. Nancy shuddered and couldn't push down the sick feeling that rose in her stomach.

She shook out the sweatshirt and held it up.

"That's Tim's. He was wearing it the night of the party," Liz said softly, staring at the big red letters—High School Varsity Band.

They could have killed him, Nancy realized, thinking of the alcohol poisoning Tim had suffered. "I can't believe this."

"And to think that Daniel knew all about this," Liz said sadly. "Why didn't he say anything?"

"Because," a voice came from behind them, "I took an oath of secrecy."

CHAPTER 13

Nancy squinted into the shadows of the doorway, where a figure was standing half in, half out of the light. Whoever it was was standing stiffly, his hands balled into fists.

"Daniel?" Liz cried out too loudly. Her voice echoed around the damp, little building.

"Hi, Liz," the voice said.

It *was* Daniel, Nancy knew. When he stepped forward, she could see the tension in his face.

"You shouldn't be down here," he said.

Nancy stepped forward. "We know your fraternity does some sort of secret initiation stuff down here, Daniel," she said quickly. "And it was involved with what happened to Tim."

Daniel raised an eyebrow. "Secret initiation?"

"Tell us what 'you have been selected' means," Nancy said.

Daniel was staring at Liz, and Nancy thought she saw him softening.

"Come on, Daniel, the truth needs to come out," Liz beseeched him.

Then Daniel's eyes became steely again. "I don't know what you're talking about," he said.

Nancy saw the panic on Liz's face and knew there was more at stake for her than the answer to the secret.

Liz lowered her eyes. "We found the missing plan," she said softly—as if she didn't really want to speak.

Daniel cocked his head. "I *still* don't know what you're talking about."

He was so convincing, Nancy almost believed him. But then she saw a flicker in his eyes, as if he was figuring it out, too, one step behind them.

"The one in the bottom drawer of your desk," Nancy said matter-of-factly.

"*My* desk?" he said, insulted.

Liz quickly stepped forward. "I was looking for something to write a note on, and I accidentally opened . . ." She couldn't finish.

Nancy lifted her hand and held the medallion they'd found up to the dim light.

Daniel matched her gaze, as if saying, So?

"The *S*," Nancy said. "It doesn't stand for 'Success,' does it? It means 'Selected.' "

Daniel glanced around as if looking for a way out. He was trapped and knew it. He shrugged. "I don't know—" he started to say.

But Nancy cut him off. "We've seen the book, Daniel. Only one pledge a year, right? And last year, that one pledge was you."

The stiffness in Daniel's posture broke, and he walked hesitantly toward the podium with the book and ran his hand over the beautiful leather.

Liz stepped forward and rested a hand on his shoulder. "Maybe it's not too late," she said.

"But it's too late for Tim," he said quietly. He took a deep breath and turned to face Nancy and Liz.

"The Select is a secret house tradition," he said. "There aren't even many Alpha Deltas who know about it. Every year, one pledge is chosen who is thought to have the strongest character, and the best possibilities of being a house leader. He's made to do a more difficult or embarrassing stunt than anyone else. But no one knows who's been picked except the other three members in the house."

"Like you," Nancy ventured an educated guess.

Daniel nodded sadly.

"But you're not the only one?" Liz asked hopefully.

"There are two more," Daniel said, his voice barely above a whisper. "Then, *afterward*, everyone finds out."

"Afterward?" Nancy said. "You mean after the stunt?"

Daniel nodded. "I was supposed to be there," he said. "But I had to be in studio."

Daniel paused and took a deep breath. "Tim's stunt was only supposed to be a joke. All they did was take his clothes and hose him down," he began.

"They?" Nancy inquired.

"Chip and John—" Daniel explained.

"Why aren't I surprised?" Nancy murmured.

"And Tim was supposed to run back to his dorm in his wet underwear, end of story. I don't know what happened afterward. Tim must have been drinking. It was just a stupid, harmless prank."

"Some prank," Liz commented sadly.

"But Chip assured me that nothing else happened. He swore it! He said that he had no idea what happened after Tim left the house in his underwear."

Nancy calmly walked over to the trunk and felt for the two empty liquor bottles. She held them up to a weak beam of moonlight filtering in through the cracked window. Nancy could see Daniel's eyes widen with surprise.

"Obviously, they thought it would be funnier to get him drunk first," Nancy said flatly. "Though my guess is that they didn't expect to make him so sick that he passed out cold—into a coma."

Nancy could hear Daniel begin to say two or three different things, but he never got far. First, he seemed doubtful, then understanding, and then plain mad.

"They lied," Daniel said angrily. He grabbed the bottles from Nancy, "I'm sorry I wasn't there."

"Daniel!" Liz called out as he stormed back through the secret door.

"Enough secrets and lies!" Daniel cried.

Nancy took off after them.

"We're gross." George laughed as she and Will lifted the last two limp pieces of leftover pizza out of the box. They were sitting on the floor of Will's living room, catching a rerun of *The President's Daughter*. Andy had just left with Reva to walk her back to her dorm, leaving party debris everywhere. But George and Will were too tired to deal with it.

"We are disgusting," Will agreed. "But it's so good."

"I know!" George laughed as she bit down on the cheesy tip.

"So Reva and Andy seem pretty pleased we're together," Will said.

A mischievous twinkle gleamed in George's eye. "After all, a ravishing woman being seen with—with the likes of you!"

Will grabbed her and twisted his face scarily, bending over like a humpback. George laughed so hard she lost her breath.

Eventually, they calmed down, and George

watched TV while Will foraged for cheese remains in the barren pizza boxes.

"But I know someone who's still not happy about us," Will said quietly.

George groaned. "Don't tell me about it. I can't get the look on Bess's face at breakfast the other day out of my mind."

"I have to admit, we didn't really handle that one too well," Will said.

"We? It's not your problem, Will. Bess is my friend—and she has a right to be mad. We always talked about sharing everything. But things change. They have to." George sighed.

Will nuzzled George in the ear. "But she still loves you," he whispered. "Bess is still your cousin."

George could feel her emotions churning. "Everything's so personal all the time with us," she said, her voice cracking a little. "And I want to keep it that way."

Will hugged her. "Maybe I'm not the one you should be telling this to," he said.

George turned in his arms. "You're smart," she said lovingly. "You're wonderful, but give me the phone now." She held out her palm as if she was waiting for change.

Laughing, Will pulled over the extension while George dialed.

"Bess?" she said. "You want to come over for—"

Will was shaking his head, shielding his eyes in mock horror—

George raised her eyebrows. "Pizza? We're starving, we've hardly eaten."

Will was already crawling across the floor to the phone to call another pizzeria that delivered.

"We can watch TV," George suggested. "Or play cards or just talk. I don't care. It's just important that we spend some time together."

George looked at Will, her eyes gleaming with pride. "And that the important people in my life get to know each other, too."

"Daniel, wait for me!" Liz called as Daniel stormed out through the passageway back to the Alpha Delta house.

Upstairs Daniel cut through the crowd with an empty liquor bottle in each fist and left behind a wake of startled people. Some conversations halted, and the noise level dropped as everyone turned to watch Daniel.

Liz and Nancy squirmed through just as Daniel was showing the bottles to Chip and John, who were standing in the corner smiling tightly.

"What are these?" Daniel asked.

Chip and John exchanged glances of mock ignorance. "Bottles?" Chip said, sending a wave of nervous laughter through the room.

"And what was in them," Daniel demanded to know.

John leaned over and took a delicate whiff. "Whew!" he said. "Serious brew!"

Liz could see a vein throbbing in Daniel's forehead, his lips set in an angry line.

"I found them in the Coop." He was seething.

John glared at him. "But, Daniel, everyone knows the Coop has been closed up for twenty years."

"Don't play this game with me," Daniel shot back. "I am a brother in this house. I know the truth about the Coop."

A few of the larger Alpha Delta brothers stepped forward, and Liz could feel her pulse quicken.

"You lied to all of us," Daniel said. "Tim is in the hospital because of you!"

Chip and John laughed nervously. John took hold of Daniel's shoulder, "You're drunk, Daniel, maybe you need some rest—"

Daniel shrugged him off. "Maybe you need to admit the truth," he challenged them. "I think we all do."

John smiled suavely. "I have no idea what you're talking about."

For a split second, Liz wondered whether Daniel *had* told them the truth. But then Nancy nudged her, and Liz saw the fear in Chip's eyes. He was nervously running his fingers through his hair.

"It was just supposed to be a prank," Daniel began. "But not to end like this." Daniel waved the bottles again. "This wasn't supposed to be a part of it. And you swore that what happened was an accident, and we all believed you!"

Chip stepped forward, his face frozen in the stupid smile of someone who was trapped. "Jeez, Daniel. You should watch what you're saying. It was just a gag, to make it harder for him to get back to his dorm," he admitted.

"Chip! Shut up!" John said.

"No," Chip said, warding John off. "It's okay. We didn't do anything wrong. We thought it was funny, and if Tim hadn't been such a baby about booze he would have been fine."

"How can you say you didn't do anything wrong," Daniel said. He shook his head. "I can't believe I wasn't there to stop you morons. I was supposed to be there. If I had been, I wouldn't have let you pour liquor into Tim."

John snorted. "Please!" he cried. "Mr. High and Mighty. You're as bad as the rest of us."

Daniel whirled around and faced him. "At least I was *worried* about Tim, while you two have been lying and scheming to save yourselves."

Daniel's voice had risen to a shout, and the silence in the room was deafening as all the partygoers listened to the argument. Liz could hear Nancy breathing heavily beside her. The other Alpha Deltas wore puzzled expressions. She could tell they were wondering about all of this.

Daniel raised his head, his gaze fixed.

"We are in danger of losing the Alpha Delta charter, and the only way to save our frat house," Daniel began calmly but firmly, "is to turn in the guilty parties."

John and Chip had fury and panic in their eyes.

"Too bad you have such a nosy girlfriend," John said to Daniel. "Too bad you forgot how to be *loyal.*"

A slow, ironic smile lifted the corners of Daniel's mouth. "I *am* loyal, John. I'm loyal to this fraternity and everything it stands for. More to the point, I'm loyal to *Tim,* who trusted us—who trusted you—and who happens to be the one lying in the hospital right now."

The fire in John's eyes went out. His resolve seemed to cave in.

"I have no idea what's going to happen to us," Daniel said, looking around the house at all the brothers and pledges. "But the important thing is what's going to happen to Tim. I don't know if the university will forgive us. But I only hope that when Tim gets better, he will."

"So that's it?" John cried. "You don't care about the house? One pledge is more important than decades of history and hundreds of alumni?"

"What about us?" Chip asked. "I suppose you're going to rat us out, too, right?"

"I'm going to tell them what I know," Daniel said quietly. "I want to show Wilder, and our friends, that we're not all goons," Daniel said. "The university is going to find out now, anyway."

Then he turned his gaze on Liz and mouthed two words—"I'm sorry."

"I'm not sure what's going to happen now," Liz whispered to Nancy, "but I have to get out of here."

Nancy knew that Liz was struggling with her feelings. She was obviously relieved that Daniel was going to tell the truth, but she was still upset that he had been involved from the beginning.

"Are you going to be okay?" Nancy asked. "Do you want me to come with you?"

Liz shrugged. "Thanks, but I think I could use some time alone." She smiled. "I'll see you back at the dorm."

Well, now what am *I* going to do? Nancy wondered as Liz left. This party's over.

As Nancy watched, everyone disappeared, talking of the confrontation that had just occurred. The Alpha Deltas were making their way downstairs, and Nancy guessed that there was about to be another meeting in the Coop. It was the only place private enough for the brothers to talk when their house was full of strangers.

Amazingly, some people had started partying again, oblivious to what had just taken place.

As Nancy stood in the middle of the room deciding what to do next, she felt a hand on her shoulder. With everything that had gone on, she was jittery, so she jumped. When she turned she found Jake standing there in a sport coat, pressed denim shirt, and jeans.

"See, I managed to get my own," he said, holding up one of the pink invitations.

"And just in time." Nancy laughed, scanning the room.

Jake looked around in mock horror. "Was it something I said?"

Nancy shrugged and beamed at him. It was the first time she'd seen him in anything but one of three or four rotating wrinkled shirts. Nancy thought he looked pretty sexy.

"All dressed up and no place to go, huh?" Nancy said, eyeing his sport coat. He'd even polished his boots.

"Looks like I missed the big climax," Jake said meaningfully. Nancy could see the questions in Jake's eyes. But he was obviously holding his reporter's nature in check, and she appreciated that. She was emotionally exhausted.

"Well, *you* look beautiful," he said, beaming. "It seems a shame to waste that outfit, since this party's turned out to be a bust. And, as you can see, I went to *great* lengths to make myself presentable."

"Are you *suggesting* something?" Nancy laughed.

"Only if you're going to say yes," Jake replied easily. "After all this effort, I don't think I could take a rejection."

"In that case," Nancy said, smiling, "maybe you better not ask. It's been a long night, and the only thing I can think about right now is crawling into bed."

Jake held his smile, but Nancy could see the disappointment behind his eyes. Nancy couldn't deny her own frustration, but she really was tired. She wanted to be alert with Jake. She didn't want to miss a thing he said.

"But listen," she said eagerly, "stop by tomorrow, and I'll fill you in on everything that happened."

"Is that a date?" Jake asked. His voice was teasing.

"A date?" she repeated, gazing back at him. Suddenly her heart started to beat faster.

Jake took a step toward her. "Tough question?"

"No," Nancy said quickly, her throat dry. "Sure, it's a date—for a meeting. If that's what you meant?" *I must be more tired than I thought,* she told herself quickly.

"That's what I meant." Jake smiled mysteriously. "A meeting. To discuss tonight's events. Remember, I've got to finish my story."

"So that's the reason you want to meet," Nancy joked.

"Oh, don't worry," Jake said, taking her hand.

He held it, studied it for a moment, and then let it drop back to her side.

"That's just my excuse." Jake grinned. "See you tomorrow then?"

"Sure," Nancy replied, unable to keep herself from grinning back. "It's a date." She waved goodbye with fingers that were still tingling.

CHAPTER 14

Kara was sitting beside Tim's bed at the hospital, trying to do some reading for a class. Outside, she heard the murmurs and shouts of students on their way to Sunday brunch. The room was bathed in morning sunlight, and Tim looked peaceful as he lay there, breathing evenly.

Tim's parents had called her the night before to let her know he had regained consciousness and would probably make a complete recovery. Kara was sitting with him while Tim's parents got some much needed rest.

Kara was only going to stay a little while, but the doctor had told her when she came in that Tim had begun to move and he might be waking up soon. So she stayed, raising her head at every sound she heard.

She was staring out the window, still on the

same page in her textbook, when she heard sounds from Tim.

Then she felt a dry hand touching hers.

Tim opened his mouth, but only managed to make a sound that sounded like gargling.

Kara helped him drink a little water to quench his parched throat.

"Thanks," Tim whispered weakly. He groaned and held his head. "Wow, do I have a headache!"

He squeezed her hand delicately and tried to smile.

"We all know what happened," Kara said. "Alpha Delt's little secret is all over campus."

Tim frowned. "I screwed up."

"Actually, you breathed new life into the whole fraternity," Kara said happily. "From this bed."

Tim shook his head. "I don't seem to be much of a fraternity man," he said.

Kara leaned closer. "I don't care, as long as you'll be my man."

"Hey, look at that!" someone cried from the doorway.

Kara turned to find Daniel, flanked by three or four other Alpha Deltas, outlined in the doorway.

Daniel moved into the room and sat on the edge of his bed. "Good morning," he joked. "Have a nice nap?"

Tim tried to smile.

Daniel leaned closer, but Kara heard every word.

"I wasn't there for you the other night," Daniel said. "I blew it and let those two jerks do this to you—"

"It's okay," Tim croaked, "It won't matter, anyway. I don't think I'm cut out for—"

Daniel held up his hand. "Don't say anything yet. What happened is not what the Alpha Delts are all about. John and Chip are going to be gone for good. The university has recommended expulsion for them. We all want you to stay in the house. We have some changes to make, and we sure could use your help."

Tim didn't answer right away. He looked at the ceiling before answering. "Let me think about it," he finally said.

Daniel patted Tim on the arm. "Think about it all you want. But no matter what you decide, I'll always be your brother. I'll never skip out on you again."

After they cleared out, Tim looked pensive.

"What do you think?" Kara asked.

Tim shrugged and turned his head. "I think about you," he said. "The last thing I really remember is walking you back to your dorm."

Kara was grinning. "That's a good place to start."

"You're doing great," Carson Drew said proudly as he stood in front of a small café near the campus, where Nancy, he, and Avery had just had Sunday brunch.

"You haven't gotten my first semester's grades yet," Nancy teased. "So the jury's still out."

Nancy, suddenly shy, glanced over to where Avery stood waiting beside her father's car. "If you don't mind my saying so, you're doing pretty well yourself."

Her father stared at her for a long moment, before holding out his arms. Nancy slid into them, and he wrapped her in a hug.

"Thank you for saying that," he whispered into her hair. "It means a lot to me that you like her."

"I do," Nancy said. "She's smart, funny—and beautiful, too."

"Now that we're talking about it, I have to admit I've been having a hard time figuring out how to feel about something you told me over brunch. I'm not sure how to feel about you and Ned," Carson admitted. "Because even though you've always been independent, it's been a long time since I've pictured you completely on your own. I guess I always thought Ned would be there for you."

"I know." Nancy sighed, leaning her head against her father's shoulder. "So did I. But actually I'm doing fine. It's amazing how things that you think will never change really can."

Carson pulled her closer.

"Except for you, of course," Nancy teased. "You'll always be my father and my very good friend."

Carson glanced over at Avery, before he looked back at his daughter. "I'm glad you know that," he said firmly, "because that *is* the one thing that will never change."

Nancy smiled and waved as her father walked back to Avery and opened the car door for her. Just before she got inside, Avery turned back and waved.

Nancy couldn't help but think how interesting it was that she and her father were at this place in their lives. She at the end of one relationship and Carson at the beginning of one.

But maybe I'm at the beginning of a new relationship, too, Nancy suddenly realized, thinking of Jake Collins. As she watched her father's car drive away, she had to laugh. Her father's life was happy and full. And so was hers.

"So, how's the Wilder on Wilder project going?" Daniel asked Liz, sitting down across the small table from where she sat in the Cave. "Will you finish it by tomorrow?"

"I'm not sure," Liz admitted, trying to figure out how she felt about Daniel. "My mind's been elsewhere. I guess you figured out that I'm doing the Alpha Delta house," Liz added.

"Yeah, I sort of got that impression." Daniel smiled. "Did you know that it was my project last year?"

"I guessed it when I took that drawing from your desk," Liz grimaced.

"Oh, right," Daniel said "Listen, about all of that—"

"You don't owe me an explanation," Liz said quickly. *I don't know if I want to hear it, anyway,* she admitted to herself.

"I realize I don't *owe* it to you," Daniel replied intently. "But I *want* you to understand. Sometimes the studio gets pretty intense. You know how badly everyone needs to blow off steam. Well, Alpha Delt was my escape from that. And I never really wanted it to be threatened. I thought I was being loyal—but there is such a thing as being too loyal. I see that now."

"Daniel, I'm sorry—" Liz began.

"But what I learned," Daniel went on quietly, "is that it's always important to make sure the friends you're being loyal to deserve that loyalty."

Liz nodded and thought about what he was saying. She might have done something similar for her suitemates.

"I'm not sure what's going to happen to the fraternity," Daniel admitted, "or to me. But I hope *we'll* still be friends."

Liz knew that Daniel was waiting for an answer. Both of them had been excited about their budding relationship, and now it seemed neither of them were sure there would be a relationship anymore.

"We'll be friends as long as you don't steal the last of the coffee," Liz joked, smiling at Daniel. "Especially tonight. I may be needing it."

Daniel nodded and stood up. He seemed relieved that she hadn't said no, although Liz thought he'd been disappointed when she said *friends*.

"Maybe I'll see you later, then," Daniel agreed. "But I can't promise about the coffee. You know at two o'clock it's a commodity more precious than gold."

Liz laughed, and watched Daniel leave with a bittersweet feeling. She wasn't ready to let things fall right back the way they'd been before, but she really didn't want to think it was over for them. She liked Daniel—a lot. And even though she'd been disappointed in him, she had to admire the way he was handling himself now.

Tonight would be a late night in the studio and Liz fully expected to be going down to the Cave for coffee. She hoped Daniel would be there, too.

Brian sat down on his bed and started flipping through the mail he'd brought up from the first-floor mail room. Junk mail went right into the garbage, and bills he stuck under his mattress. Unfortunately, they never actually disappeared, and once a month he had to pull them all out and write checks.

Finally all the mail had been accounted for, except for one white envelope with his name printed on the front. There was no return address. Sweat broke out on his brow as he tore open the plain white envelope and a small piece of paper fluttered out. Brian's hand was shaking as he picked the paper up off the floor.

I'm still waiting for my $$$. I wonder why? If you don't cough it up soon, you'll be very sorry.

Brian crumpled the letter and threw it across the room. Then he jumped up and started pacing, shaking with anger and something more. Fear.

What am I going to do? he wondered desperately.

"So, that's it." Nancy smiled, cupping her coffee in her hands as she watched Jake scribble down the last of the story she'd dictated to him about Tim and the Alpha Deltas.

Jake had met Nancy at Java Joe's for a jolt of caffeine after she'd said goodbye to her father. He wanted to get going on the article for the next day's paper.

"I bet that felt great." Jake smiled, looking up and gazing at Nancy. "I mean, pushing open that door to the Coop and knowing you'd discovered some great secret."

"Well," Nancy agreed, "it was exciting, but it was also kind of sad because of Tim."

"Yeah," Jake agreed. "That's true. Well, he seems to be okay now."

"So does my roommate." Nancy chuckled. "She hasn't had the greatest of luck with guys, and I was beginning to worry that she thought the whole thing was her fault."

"So what do you think will happen to the fraternity?" Jake asked, closing the cover of his notebook and putting it away.

Nancy smiled. It was nice to know the "interview" was at an end, and that Jake was interested in having a regular conversation.

"My guess is that John Reed and Chip Booth will probably be expelled. But I don't know about the rest of them. I don't think they all deserve to get in trouble."

"The fraternity'll get probation from the university for sure," Jake commented. "Which might mean no more parties this year. But if they all come clean like Daniel, I doubt the whole fraternity will be kicked off campus."

"I hope not," Nancy said, taking another sip of hot coffee. She also couldn't help but wonder what would happen with Daniel and Liz. Would their relationship be able to survive this? Nancy knew Liz had been really hurt over Daniel's involvement, and especially because Tim had been a friend of his.

"You look serious all of a sudden," Jake remarked, cocking his head.

"Oh, I'm just thinking about Liz," Nancy admitted. "I was wondering how they'll get along now."

"That's exactly why I stayed out of the whole thing," Jake deadpanned. "I didn't want it to hurt our relationship."

Nancy laughed. "Oh, right—okay. But what do you mean, our *relationship?*"

"Well, actually," he admitted, "I mean the future of our relationship."

Suddenly she was unable to ignore the little skip in her heart. "Which is?" she asked.

"Which is—I'm not exactly sure." Jake said. "But I'm up for finding out. It needs a lot more investigation."

Nancy laughed at Jake. He made her laugh. He might be a little rough around the edges, but he meant well. And it was pretty clear he had a big heart—one that seemed to be beating as quickly at hers.

Nancy smiled innocently. "Anything I can do?"

"Actually, yes," Jake replied dryly. "There's a play coming up, I'm sure you've heard of it. The wonderfully entertaining musical *Grease!* Maybe we can see it together?"

"Are you sure that's allowed?" Nancy asked. "I mean, upperclass reporter and lowly freshman? There aren't any rules about that?"

Jake shrugged. "You know what they say," he said.

"What do they say?"

Jake gazed at her and became suddenly serious. "That rules are made to be broken."

Nancy felt her face heat up. But she returned Jake's look head on. "I like the sound of that."

NEXT IN NANCY DREW ON CAMPUS™:

How do you keep cool when life is getting hotter by the minute? That's the question Nancy's asking, and she's having a tough time finding an answer. Like Bess, television star Casey Fontaine is pledging Kappa, and the whole sorority is in an uproar. The reason is, Casey's getting special treatment, and there could be an investigation . . . meaning Kappa is in serious danger of losing its charter. Meanwhile, the drama department's first play is opening, and Bess and Brian are in the cast. But someone's threatening to reveal a secret that could make Brian an outcast with his family. Nancy's offered to help, while dealing with a dilemma of her own. Lately romance has spelled trouble, and she wants to cool it. But with all the moves Jake is making, she's feeling the heat . . . in *It's Your Move*, Nancy Drew on Campus #6.

REAL LIFE

I've had it with being An-ying.
From now on. . .

CALL ME CATHY

by Margaret Meacham

I thought the nightmare would never end. . .

MY BEST FRIEND DIED

by Alan Gelb

Maybe my best friend was right.
Maybe I was crazy. . .

HELP ME!

by Wendy Corsi Staub

An Archway Paperback
Published by Pocket Books

1067-02